Warning:

This book is about one of life's natural processes that is an important part of health and wellbeing.

So … if you don't fart,
Don't Read This Book!

But if you like to let one rip …
blow on in!

Also by Andy Jones

The Enormous Book of Hot Jokes for Kool Kids

The FART-ionary

ANDY JONES

Illustrated by
DAVID PUCKERIDGE

ABC
Books

The ABC 'Wave' device is a trademark of the
Australian Broadcasting Corporation and is used
under licence by HarperCollins*Publishers* Australia.

First published in Australia in 2011
by HarperCollins*Publishers* Australia Pty Limited
ABN 36 009 913 517
harpercollins.com.au

HarperCollins*Publishers*
Level 13, 201 Elizabeth Street, Sydney NSW 2000, Australia
31 View Road, Glenfield, Auckland 0627, New Zealand
A 53, Sector 57, Noida, UP, India
77–85 Fulham Palace Road, London W6 8JB, United Kingdom
2 Bloor Street East, 20th floor, Toronto, Ontario M4W 1A8, Canada
10 East 53rd Street, New York NY 10022, USA

National Library of Australia Cataloguing-in-Publication entry:

Jones, Andy, 1961–
   The fartionary / Andy Jones; illustrated by David Puckeridge.
   ISBN: 978 0 7333 3056 8 (pbk.)
   For children.
   Flatulence–Juvenile fiction.
   Puckeridge, David.
   Australian Broadcasting Corporation.
A828.302

Cover and internal design by Pigs Might Fly
Cover images by Pigs Might Fly
Author cartoon on page 252 by Olga Ho
Typeset in Berkeley Oldstyle Book by Pigs Might Fly
Printed and bound in Australia by Griffin Press
70gsm Classic used by HarperCollins*Publishers* is a natural, recyclable product made
from wood grown in sustainable forests. The manufacturing processes conform to the
environmental regulations in the country of origin, Finland.

5 4 3 2 1   11 12 13 14

To John and Gisela Jones,
who both knew the value of the passage of time and wind!

A. JONES

CONTENTS

FARTS & FLUFFS IN HISTORY

SCIENCE IN THE SEAT OF YOUR PANTS

ANIMAL CRACKERS

FARTS 'N' PHYSICS

FARTY FOODS

A FART BY ANY OTHER NAME

FARTY
FACTS

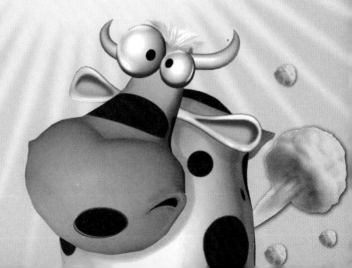

FARTOLOGY
The biology of the fart

A fart is a mixture of gases. (You already knew that, didn't you!)

But where do these gases come from?

Well, there are a few places …

- air we swallow
- gas made in our stomach and intestines

Let's start with the first one. When you eat or drink, air is taken in with each mouthful as well. If you eat a large amount of food, eat quickly or even talk while you are eating, you will swallow lots of air.

Once this food and air reaches your stomach, it starts being digested. Imagine your stomach as a human washing machine – the food gets churned up and broken down until it's nice and soupy. (Mmm, stomach soup!) It then moves through the small intestine into the large intestine.

But what happens then? The food that hasn't been digested yet is attacked by bacteria in the large intestine. While these bacteria are hard at work breaking down the leftover food, they produce lots of gas.

Now for the good bit!!!

Apart from burping, the only way for the swallowed air and gas to get out of your body is through your bottom.

And that's how we get the birth of … the 'Bottom Burp'!

FARTS IN MOTION
How farts travel through the body

A fart travels through your body the same way that food does.

When you take a bite of a sandwich and swallow it, it moves through your digestive system via something called … (medical term alert!) 'peristalsis'.

A good way to explain peristalsis is to grab your sausage doorstop. You know, that long snaky thing that sits at the bottom of your back door to stop the wind and creepy-crawlies getting in. Pick it up and, starting at one end, squeeze it hand over hand along the length of the sausage. This action is exactly like what happens automatically in your body as soon as you eat … peristalsis!

Peristalsis pushes the food and air that you swallow down to your stomach. Some of the swallowed air is released by burping, but the rest travels down into your intestines. More gas is created in the intestines by the hard-working bacteria in there. And where does this leftover air and gas go?

It gets propelled through your intestines until it POPS out through your bottom!

THE STINKING TRUTH
Why farts smell

Farts smell as a result of what we eat.

Most of the gases produced in our bodies (like carbon dioxide, hydrogen, methane and nitrogen) don't have any smell. But there's one gas – hydrogen sulfide – that is super stinky! Hydrogen sulfide is sometimes called 'rotten egg gas' because that's what it smells like – stinky, disgusting rotten eggs!

You need sulfur to create hydrogen sulfide. Which means the more sulfur your diet contains, the stinkier your fluffs will be!

Meat, eggs, garlic, cabbage, broccoli, cauliflower and milk are all high in sulphur – so they are perfect for producing super stinky stenches!

Beans (like lentils and chickpeas) often cause loud fluffs that don't smell that much. For example, lentil soup is well known to give you lots of gas that isn't too smelly and is often fun to let rip!

Farty Tip #1: Eat lentil soup to perform a bottom-burp concert that won't stink out your family and friends!

THE SPHINCTER SYMPHONY
The sound of the sulfur orchestra!

The noise of a fart will depend on the tightness of your bottom muscles. It will also depend on the speed of the fart and the amount of gas being produced. Generally, the bigger the fart, the louder it will be!

Have you ever noticed that your farts sound louder when you're sitting on the toilet? Or that they sound high and squeaky when you're squeezing your bottom muscles?

Farts can make lots of different sounds. They can be explosive, squeaky, thunderous, poppy and squelchy! They can also be long or short and have changes in pitch. With enough practice, even 'Jingle Bells' can be squeezed out!

All in all, everyone has an orchestra in their bottom with a multitude of sounds, tones and textures – high notes, low notes and percussive sounds. Some people can even make special-effects sounds: rumbles, slaps, leaking balloons, squeaks, squawks and squirts.

So tune up and let the concert begin!

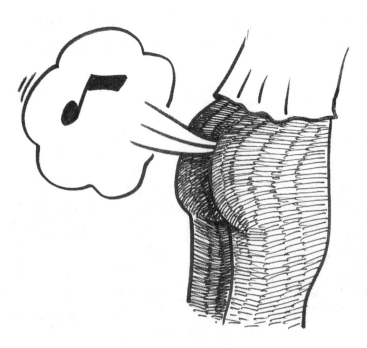

THE FART FACT FILE
True or false?

FF1 – The scientific name for farting is 'flatulence'.

TRUE! And the scientific name for the gas produced in the stomach and intestines is 'flatus'.

FF2 – Some people never ever fart.

FALSE! Every human being farts!! If they say they don't fart, they are fibbing – big time! (You can even fart after you die!)

FF3 – Boys fart more than girls.

FALSE! We all fart around the same amount, but boys are more likely to fart in public and in front of their friends (because it's funny … apparently!).

FF4 – The average person farts around 10 to 15 times a day.

TRUE! Although, this depends on what you have eaten and how much air you have swallowed.

FF5 – Girls don't fart.

FALSE! Lies lies lies!!!! Every human being farts!

FF6 – Famous people don't fart.

FALSE! Doctors, lawyers, pop stars, actors, politicians, bus drivers and even *teachers* fart! (Hee hee!)

FF7 – You fart more in the morning.

FALSE! It's different for everyone. Some people fart more in the morning and some fart more as they are going to sleep at night. Almost everyone farts more after meals.

FF8 – Girls' farts are smellier than boys'.

FALSE! Whether a fart is smelly or not depends on what you have eaten, not on whether you are a boy or a girl.

FF9 – Some farts are odourless to begin with and then start to smell.

FALSE! If a fart has a smell, it will be there straightaway – it might just take a few seconds for it to assault your nostrils!

FF10 – A fart is just a burp that comes out the wrong end.

FALSE! A burp comes from the stomach and is usually made up of fewer gases than a fart.

FF11 – Chewing gum makes you fart more.

TRUE! Chewing gum makes you swallow more air and therefore causes more bubbalicious butt blow-offs!

FF12 – If you hold a fart in too long, it will kill you.

FALSE! If you hold in a fart during the day, it will most likely pop out as soon as you relax or fall asleep at night. So the only person it might harm is the person next to you when it eventually seeps out!

THE DANGER OF HOLDING IT IN

FF13 – When you hold in a fart, it disappears.

FALSE! When you hold in a fart, it travels back up your intestines ... only to stink its way out later!

FF14 – Farts are louder first thing in the morning.

TRUE *and* **FALSE!** There is no evidence that farts are louder at a certain time of the day. Your farts might *seem* louder in the morning if you launch them in the bathroom, because the sound will reverberate off the bathroom tiles. This type of fart is known as 'Morning Thunder'!

FF15 – Baked beans make you fart.

TRUE! Baked beans can make you fart like a popcorn-popping machine! The reason is that baked beans have a certain type of sugar in them that is hard for humans to digest. When this sugar reaches our intestines, the bacteria in there go berserk and make lots of gas.

FARTY TRIVIA

Break wind

The polite way of talking about farting is to say 'break wind'. Back in the 16th century, people used this expression to describe both burping and farting. And guess what? It's still used to describe farting today!

Gone with the wind

Did you know that we swallow around 300 times per day? Each time we swallow, we take in around three millilitres of air. And the more air we take in, the more windy pops we do!

Gulp

The medical term for swallowing too much air is 'aerophagia' (pronounced air-o-fay-gia). Aerophagia happens when people eat a lot of chewing gum, drink too many fizzy drinks or eat too quickly. People also swallow air when they are nervous or stressed. *(I have a spelling test this morning … GULP!!)* And we all know the more air we swallow … the more babbling butt blow-offs!

Billions of bacteria

Did you know that there are 400 different types of bacteria in your intestines? And the total number of individual bacteria in there is around 100 BILLION! (Wow! That's a lot of bacteria. I hope they all get on!!)

FARTY POEM

Musical Farts

A. JONES

Farting can be musical

Everyone can play

A tune can be created

Each and every day.

FARTING ETIQUETTE

THE DO's AND DON'Ts OF THE BABBLING BOTTOM

Even though farting is a natural part of life, there are still some do's and don'ts when it comes to this noisy, gassy bodily function. I call them the 'Rule of bum'! (Ha!)

When not to ... (farting no-go zones!)

- Never let one rip at the dinner table. (Ewwww!!!)

- Never let one go in front of guests (unless they are visiting Fart Doctors!).

- Never let one go when you are giving a speech in front of a large group of people.

- Never let one go in a bank (people might mistake the sound for a gunshot and think you are robbing the bank!).

- Never let one rip when you are trying to impress a new girlfriend or boyfriend.

- Never let one rip in the principal's office (or else your butt gas won't be the only thing that gets expelled! Hahahaha!).

- Never let out a squeaker when you are meeting your girlfriend or boyfriend's father for the first time. HOLD IT IN!

- Never let one go when you are meeting your girlfriend or boyfriend's mother for the first time. She won't think you're a lovely boy/girl!

The main 'rule of bum' is that you don't let your bottom babble in front of people who might be offended by the sound or smell. (Remember, some people like to keep their butt blasts private!)

When to ...
(farting safety zones!)

• It's okay to do a butt bomb when you are on your own.

• It's okay when you are in the bath.

• It's okay at a footy game (any LOUD sounds will be covered up by all the screaming and shouting!).

• It's okay when you are outdoors (especially if there's lots of open space around you).

• It's okay when you are at the beach or swimming in the ocean.

- It's okay in a doctor's surgery. Doctors are trained to deal with all types of bodily functions. There is nothing your doctor hasn't seen (or smelled!) before. If you do let one rip, your doctor probably won't even react!

- It's okay when you are with friends (especially if you're at a Farty Party!).

Farty Tip #2: If you are in public and you absolutely have to let one go, make sure it's an SBD (Silent But Deadly) so no one can hear it!

FARTY TRIVIA
Farty pants

An American company has invented special underpants to help people who fart more than usual or whose farts are particularly stinky. (Remember, it's normal to fart around 10 to 15 times per day!) The underpants have a built-in filter which is meant to get rid of any nasty odours. The makers of the special underpants (called 'Under-Ease') say their undies 'relieve the pain without the shame'. (That sounds a bit like a nappy to me!!!)

FARTING FIBS
What to say if you let one go in public!

Everyone has been in the situation where they have let one go in public and been embarrassed because it was so smelly.

Here are some excuses that are guaranteed to get you out of even the stinkiest situation!

The doggy doo excuse

'Can you smell that? Woah! Someone must have stepped in doggy doo …'
(The perfect excuse if you let one loose in a group.)

The curry excuse

'Oops … That one just slipped out. Must be the curry I ate last night.'
(Use this excuse when you can't blame anyone else!)

The dog excuse

'Ahh, Rover, you stink! I better buy you a different brand of dog food.'
(You can use this at home or when walking your dog.)

The cat excuse

'That smelly little cat! What a little stinker!!!'
(You can blame the cat any time!)

The old lady excuse

'I can't believe that old lady just let one go!
Unbelievable!'
(You can use this at shops, train stations, airports or
nursing homes.)

The blame it on your
buddy excuse

'It wasn't me ... Did you do that? Pheww-eee!
That stinks!'
(You can use this any time you are with your friends.)

The lift excuse

There's no need to say anything at all with this excuse! Just edge away from the person next to you in the lift and raise your eyebrows!

The weather excuse

'Did you hear that thunder? There must be a storm coming …'
(If you let out an ear-splitting butt bomb, blame the weather!)

The petrol excuse

'Phew! That unleaded petrol stinks like rotten eggs!'
(You can use this if you're in the car and one pops out.)

The budgie excuse

'Wow! I didn't know that budgie farts smelled
that bad!'

(You can use this when you are standing near a bird cage.)

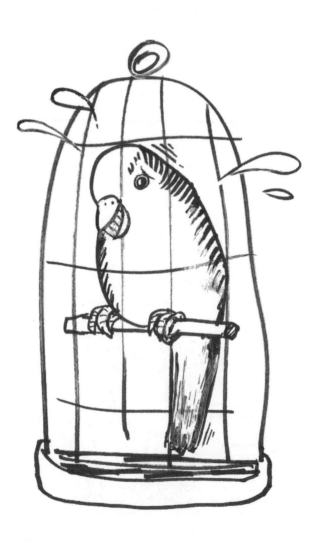

FARTY POEM

Marty Farty

ANONYMOUS

Marty Farty

Had a party

All the gang were there

Mr Hopper

Blew a whopper

All went out for air!

FARTS &
FLUFFS
IN
HISTORY

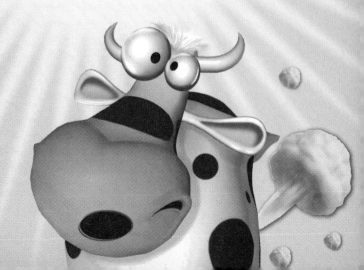

FARTISTORY
Farts in history

As long as humans and animals have existed, there have been farts. Farting has been around forever – in all cultures, tribes and societies.

What do ...

Cleopatra, Alexander the Great, Leonardo da Vinci, Shakespeare, Captain Cook, Ned Kelly, Sir Donald Bradman, Albert Einstein, Ian Thorpe, Michael Clarke and even the Queen of England ...

have in common?

The answer is that all of these people have created history by doing amazing things ...

AND ...

all of them (yes, all of them!) have farted in their lives!!

Remember that no matter who you are and what you do in life, if you eat, you fart ... and that's that!

Farting in the ancient Arab world

Historical records tell us that in the ancient Arab world you were allowed to break wind in public, but if it had a strong smell you could get yourself in big, big trouble … especially if you stank up the room in the company of royalty! This person was called a *Fezwaun* (or 'Fizzler') and he or she could be executed if the fart was thought to be smelly enough! (I wonder if they ate eggs back then??)

Shakespeare and farting

William Shakespeare was born in 1564. Some people think he was the greatest storyteller of all time. But guess what? Shakespeare makes reference to 'breaking wind' in one of his plays!

Shakespeare writes:

*'A man may **break** a word with you, sir; and words are but **wind**; Ay, and **break it in your face**, so he **break it not behind**.'*

(From the play *The Comedy of Errors*)

Farting in World War II

Rumour has it that during World War II scientists were working on ways to turn farting into a weapon. Apparently, they used to ask soldiers to eat large amounts of baked beans so they could study the fart gas!!!

Farty Tip #3: When breaking wind in public, tell people you are perfecting a new secret weapon for the government!

DANGER
TESTING RANGE

"3... 2... 1..."

FAMOUS FARTERS
History's most extraordinary fluffers

Fartomaniac

Every now and then, history produces an individual who is so incredibly talented they write themselves into the hearts, minds and, in this case, *noses* of everyone. So let us stand in awe (or should I say *smell* in awe) of the man named Joseph Pujol. (Funnily enough, his surname is pronounced *Poo-Shol*!)

Mr Pujol was a gifted French performer who went by the stage name of 'Le Pétomane' (which roughly translates as 'Fartomaniac'). With a name like that, it's obvious what Mr Pujol was gifted at!

The story goes that Le Pétomane had practised long and hard and even endured extreme pain to train his sphincter muscles (which are muscles in your bottom). His bottom was so well trained he could make his farts sound like a flute and even played well-known French songs in tune! (I wonder how many orchestras today have farty flautists?)

Le Pétomane liked to imitate thunderstorms, animal sounds and even cannon fire with his farts. (Now that's what I call a weapon – a real 'gas bum gun'!)

Le Pétomane could also blow out a candle by farting in its direction from 30 centimetres away. Well, that certainly gives a new meaning to the words 'blowing your own trumpet'!

In 1892, Le Pétomane starred at the famous Moulin Rouge in Paris. He became the most popular performer of his day. At his shows, some people laughed so hard they fainted and had to be treated by nurses who were stationed around the theatre. The nurses were armed with smelling salts to revive the 'faint-hearted' (or should that be 'faint-*farted*'?!).

Mr Methane

There is another famous farter who was born long after Le Pétomane. In fact, he is still performing shows today! He goes by the name of Mr Methane. (Methane is one of the gases that is found in farts.)

Mr Methane was born in Macclesfield, Cheshire in England. (**Interesting farty fact:** England is the baked bean capital of the world!)

Apparently, Mr Methane discovered his special talent for farting at the age of fifteen when he was doing yoga. He ran to school the next day and squeezed out twenty farts in less than a minute for his group of friends. (Wow! That's what I call 'rapid-fire farting'!)

Mr Methane's act became so popular that he turned into a 'professional farter'. When Mr Methane performs, he dresses like a caped crusader. He wears a green and purple costume and looks a bit like Superman or Spider-Man. (I wonder if spiders fart??)

In 2009, Mr Methane even auditioned for the show *Britain's Got Talent*. He told the judges that he wanted to put the 'art into fart'. He held a microphone to his backside and started performing *The Blue Danube* waltz with his bottom! Unfortunately, the judges didn't agree with him and all three of them buzzed him off the show in less than two minutes.

Obviously, Mr Methane is a big fan of the original French 'father of farting', Le Pétomane. He says that he uses the same techniques as Le Pétomane. After performing on many TV and radio shows, Mr Methane is certainly doing his explosive best to promote the lost art of 'singing with your bottom'!!

FARTY TRIVIA
Record-breaking raspberries

The longest single fart ever recorded was by Bernard Clemmens of London, England. Bernard's fart lasted for a whole 2 minutes and 42 seconds!! (That's a long time to let one *riiiiiiiiip*!!!!)

Oldest (and smelliest!) word

Did you know that the word 'fart' is one of the oldest words in the English language? It can be traced back to the Old English word 'feortan' (which means 'to break wind').

Her Royal Fartness!

Apparently, Queen Victoria of England liked to eat her food quickly, so she was well-known for her farting! So next time you let loose, just say you are doing an impression of good old Queen Vic!

FARTY POEM

Long Lost Fart ...

ANONYMOUS

It is better to have farted and lost

Than never to have farted at all!

SCIENCE
IN THE
SEAT OF
YOUR
PANTS

FART CHARTS
Graphs for gaseous studies

The Fart Chart and Food Chart are a way to collect important information relating to your farts. For example, how many times a day you fart, which foods make you fart more – and, of course, what *type* of farts you do!

You may have noticed that some days you will be a little more 'windy' than others. There is always a scientific reason for this. With the help of the Fart Chart and Food Chart, you will be able to record all the relevant information and then identify any patterns or unusually 'windy' behaviour!

The Fart Chart and Food Chart will tell you …

- The number of times you fart per day
- The number of times you fart per week
- The time of the day (morning, afternoon, night) when you fart the most
- What you have eaten before a farting episode
- The types of foods that might increase farting

You will need a notepad and pen to collect the information each day and then you can add it to your Fart Chart and Food Chart each night.

NOTE: You don't need to record any farts when you are going to the toilet – those farts don't count!

Food Chart

Step 1: Look at the sample Food Chart on page 54. You can either draw up your own Food Chart (using felt-tip pens and a piece of cardboard), or photocopy the blank Food Chart from page 58. Stick your Food Chart somewhere you will see it every day. (For example, on your wardrobe door!)

Step 2: Each day, write down everything you eat on the Food Chart (and I mean absolutely *everything*!). Every little bit of food you eat (including morning tea, afternoon tea and snacks) has to be written down to make sure the Food Chart is accurate. (Remember, we are searching for the scientific truth here!) That means every sandwich, biscuit, lolly, banana, muesli bar and piece of chewing gum has to be recorded on your Food Chart. Then you will be able to study the information you have collected at the end of the week.

Fart Chart

Step 1: Look at the sample Fart Chart on page 56. You can either make your own Fart Chart (using felt-tip pens and a piece of cardboard), or photocopy the blank Fart Chart from page 60. Keep your Fart Chart near your Food Chart!

Step 2: Each day, record the number of farts you do by drawing them on the Fart Chart. You can also record the type of fart you do, by using the Fart Key below.

Fart Key

NF   Normal Fart
SBD Silent But Deadly
EB   Egg Bomb (*ewwww!*)
BBB Baked Bean Bang (loud but not smelly)
MG   Machine Gun (lots of little farts one after the other)
TT   Thunder Thud (the biggest, baddest fart of all!)

Now that you've drawn up your charts …
go Fartologists, go!!

SAMPLE FOOD CHART

Monday	Tuesday	Wednesday	Thursday
Breakfast	**Breakfast**	**Breakfast**	**Breakfast**
• 2 boiled eggs with toast soldiers, orange juice, glass of Milo • Muesli bar, 4 caramel buds	• 2 Weetbix with banana and milk, orange juice, toast with baked beans • 2 cheese sticks		
Lunch	**Lunch**	**Lunch**	**Lunch**
• Ham and cheese sandwich, apple juice, chocolate cupcake • Grilled cheese on toast, pineapple juice	• Chicken, lettuce and mayonnaise sandwich, orange juice, fruit sticks • Milo		
Dinner	**Dinner**	**Dinner**	**Dinner**
• Chicken schnitzel, mashed potatoes and beans, ice-cream with peaches • Hot chocolate	• Lentil soup, sausages with fried onions and cabbage, stewed apples and prunes with ice-cream		

Friday	Saturday	Sunday
Breakfast	Breakfast	Breakfast
Lunch	Lunch	Lunch
Dinner	Dinner	Dinner

SAMPLE FART CHART

Monday	Tuesday	Wednesday	Thursday
Breakfast	**Breakfast**	**Breakfast**	**Breakfast**
NF NF EB EB EB	NF NF BBB		
Lunch	**Lunch**	**Lunch**	**Lunch**
NF NF	NF NF SBD!		
Dinner	**Dinner**	**Dinner**	**Dinner**
SBD! MG	TT TT MG TT TT TT TT TT		

Friday	Saturday	Sunday
Breakfast	Breakfast	Breakfast
Lunch	Lunch	Lunch
Dinner	Dinner	Dinner

Fart Key

NF Normal Fart
SBD Silent But Deadly
EB Egg Bomb
BBB Baked Bean Bang (loud but not smelly)
MG Machine Gun (lots of little farts one after the other)
TT Thunder Thud (the biggest, baddest fart of all!)

FOOD CHART (for photocopying)

Monday	Tuesday	Wednesday	Thursday
Breakfast	Breakfast	Breakfast	Breakfast
Lunch	Lunch	Lunch	Lunch
Dinner	Dinner	Dinner	Dinner

Friday	Saturday	Sunday
Breakfast	Breakfast	Breakfast
Lunch	Lunch	Lunch
Dinner	Dinner	Dinner

FART CHART (for photocopying)

Monday	Tuesday	Wednesday	Thursday
Breakfast	Breakfast	Breakfast	Breakfast
Lunch	Lunch	Lunch	Lunch
Dinner	Dinner	Dinner	Dinner

Friday	Saturday	Sunday
Breakfast	Breakfast	Breakfast
Lunch	Lunch	Lunch
Dinner	Dinner	Dinner

Fart Key

NF Normal Fart
SBD Silent But Deadly
EB Egg Bomb
BBB Baked Bean Bang
(loud but not
smelly)
MG Machine Gun
(lots of little farts
one after the
other)
TT Thunder Thud
(the biggest,
baddest fart of
all!)

BOTTOM BUBBLES
H_2O farts

Have you ever been relaxing in a bath or swimming pool and released a 'bottom bubble'? I'm sure most of you have!

Now ... the bottom bubble is more than a just bubble, it's actually visible science. Yes, that's right! When you are in water you can see the result of gas being released from your body, so the bottom bubble doubles as a science experiment. (As well as being a little personal moment shared between you and your gastrointestinal system!)

A few questions ...

- What is the bubble made up of?
- Why does the released gas form a bubble and rise to the surface?
- Does the bubble smell?

Answers ...

- The bottom bubble is just a fart trapped in water – and a fart is a mixture of gases (including air and other gases).
- When you release a bottom bubble in the bath, the water traps the gases together in a ball (or bubble). These gases are lighter than water, so the bubble will rise up to the surface where it ... pops!
- The bubble bottom is unlikely to smell while it's still under water, but as soon as it rises to the surface and pops, it will release its stench into the atmosphere.

Who thought farting could be so scientific?!

Bottom bubble experiments (BBEs)

BBE #1: This is an experiment to do on your own. Hop in the bath and get comfy ... Now slowly release a bottom bubble. Watch how it pops and explodes as the gas hits the surface!

BBE #2: This experiment is the same as the first one, but you have to try to catch the bottom bubble as it hits the surface. You can either use your hands to catch it (hold them in a cup shape) or a plastic bottle to trap the bubble. Once you've trapped it, have a sniff. The smell will depend on what you have eaten. (Ewwww ... Eggy!!!!)

BBE #3: This is a group experiment, preferably done in a swimming pool. You will need goggles or snorkel masks, and also a group of friends who really want to see science at work! You can take turns being the bottom-bubble blower depending on who's ready to let one fly. The other people need to dive underwater and give the thumbs-up signal to the person releasing the butt bomb. Then watch and be amazed … The gas is squeezed out in a bubble which quickly floats to the surface. Now, if you and your friends are true daredevils you can have a sniff as the bubble explodes into the air … (Be brave!!)

FARTY POEM

Gust of Wind

ANONYMOUS

A belch is but a gust of wind

That cometh from the heart

But if it takes a downward turn

It then becomes a fart!

ANIMAL CRACKERS

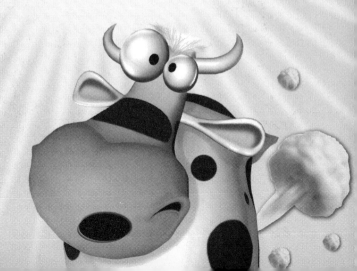

WHICH ANIMALS DO ... AND WHICH DON'T!

Science holds the answer to which animals fart and which don't! As we know, farts come from swallowed air and from gas produced in our stomach and intestines. (Together, the stomach and intestines are called 'guts'.) This air and gas travels through our guts towards our bottoms where it pops out as a fart!

Okay, the key word here is 'guts'. Animals with guts are capable of farting.

But do all animals have guts? The answer is a big whopping NO!!!!

Let's look at the animals on the next page ...

Sea sponges

Sea sponges look like plants, but they are actually one of the world's simplest animals. A sea sponge is covered with tiny holes (called 'pores') and it feeds on the nutrients in seawater. A sea sponge is made up of just a few different types of cells – it doesn't have a heart, brain, stomach or intestines (so no guts!).

So … because a sea sponge doesn't have any guts, it can't fart!

Jellyfish

Guess what? Jellyfish are not actually fish! They belong to a group of animals called 'invertebrates' (which means they don't have a backbone). The body of a jellyfish is shaped like a bell (or umbrella) with tentacles attached. A jellyfish has no heart, brain, eyes, liver or guts, but it does have a mouth. Food is taken in through the mouth – and then the leftovers are pushed out through the same opening!

That means a jellyfish can 'burp' (sort of), but it can't fart!

"Jellyfish did it."

Giant tube worms

These amazing animals live on the sea floor near active volcanoes. They can grow up to 2.4 metres long. They are covered with feathery growths made up of over 200,000 tiny tentacles.

But a giant tube worm has no mouth, stomach or intestines!

So how can it live then? Well, scientists believe that hundreds of BILLIONS of bacteria live inside the worm. The worm absorbs gases (like oxygen) from seawater directly through its skin. The bacteria then turn these gases into food for the worm. The relationship between the bacteria and the worm is called ... (scientific term alert!) 'symbiosis', because they depend on each other for survival.

The worms live without ever eating (as we know it). What a life!

So the verdict is ... no mouth, no stomach, no intestines ... no fart!!!!

FARTY FUNNY

Q: Why couldn't the skeleton fart?

A: *He didn't have the guts!*

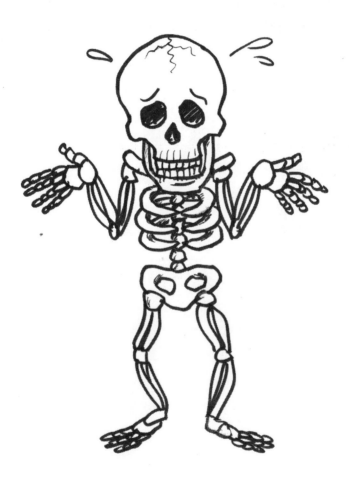

THE ANIMAL KINGDOM'S SMELLIEST!

Now we know that any animal with a stomach and intestines (or 'guts') can fart, we can identify the most stinky!

Snake Apparently these slithering reptiles pack an awful stink many times bigger than their size!

Lizard Another smelly reptile … Lizards use their farts as a defensive weapon. (And you thought that was only skunks, didn't you?!)

Dog I know that you know that dogs can release some eye-watering stink bombs! (It's because of their diet. Canned dog food is a major gas-producing culprit!)

Tortoise The giant land tortoise lives for a very long time. Apparently, its farts also take a long time to ferment (just like ginger beer!). But when a giant land turtle releases a fart, it can reduce adults to tears!

Lion The king of the jungle is ranked Number 5 on the stinky scale! (The culprit is undigested raw meat!)

Bear Bears are big and they eat big … And yes, bears fart big, too! Imagine the first fart after hibernating for six months! (Phewwwwww-eee!!!!!)

Pig They say you haven't lived until you are downwind of a pig passing wind. (Pigs eat anything and everything!)

Chicken The chicken can let one rip like no other bird! This plucky clucky edible delight not only produces eggs, but one of the stinkiest gases of all! (Question: Do chickens eat eggs or just lay them??)

Cow Cows have a stomach with four compartments so they have an advantage over other animals – more gas-making machines! As a result, cows fart more than most animals. They produce a huge amount of methane gas, which scientists tell us is one of the causes of global warming. (Apparently, just one cow gives off around

200 litres of methane gas in a single day!)

Elephant These animals deserve a special mention.
The mother of all mammals apparently blows out more
farts than any other animal in the wild.

Termite Now, you might think because of the tiny
size of the termite it couldn't possibly do any damage in
the stench stakes. Well, recent research says that termites
produce LOADS of methane gas – maybe even more than

all of our cars, planes and factories put together! This is because termites eat wood and need lots of bacteria in their guts to help them digest it. (Is there such a thing as a wood hamburger??)

Conclusion While cows produce the most methane gas overall, termites produce the most methane gas for their size!

PERFUME EAU la STINK!

Have you ever noticed that some of the things that we think are smelly and disgusting seem like perfume to animals?

Take dogs, for example. A dog's sense of smell is around one thousand times more sensitive than a human's. But dogs eat and smell some pretty questionable things (like farts!) and seem to really enjoy it.

So why are dogs attracted to things that smell bad?

While there are lots of theories, no one knows for sure!

MOO MOO POO POO
Farting cows

Now, we know that termites make more methane gas than any other creature for their size, but cows are still the Number 1 methane-gas-producing fart machines on the planet! (Sheep also add a considerable amount of methane gas to the fart-and-burp pool.)

Imagine a happy cow standing in a paddock, slowly nibbling on the green grass beneath her hooves … It makes a pretty picture, doesn't it? But while this big-eyed, milkshake-making dairy cow blissfully chews her way across a paddock, she is actually having a big effect on the Earth's atmosphere!

Here's the reason why. That lovely, super juicy green grass goes in the cow at one end (mouth), then is churned through a stomach with four compartments!* In the first compartment live BILLIONS of bacteria, which help the cow digest the grass. But bacteria also produce lots of methane gas, which is why cows burp and fart so much.

* An animal that has a stomach divided into four compartments is called a 'ruminant'.

In fact, scientists now think more methane gas comes out of cows as *burps* than it does as farts. (Hey, that's a great name for a rock band – The Burping Bovines!)

Like the old song says, 'up, up and away …' Once the methane gas is burped or farted out of the cow, it floats slowly up into the atmosphere.

Now, it's natural to have some methane gas (along with other gases) in the atmosphere. These gases act like a 'blanket' around the Earth, trapping in the heat from the sun and keeping the Earth nice and warm.

But when the amount of gases gets too high, the 'blanket' becomes too thick and the planet heats up. This is called 'global warming'.

Think back to our happily grazing cow. Do you think she knows she might be damaging the Earth's atmosphere and contributing to global warming? I think not. Miss Moo probably has no idea that her gaseous methane releases are even happening!

To prove my point, here is some dialogue taken from Miss Moo in her paddock.

Miss Moo: *Buurrrrp* … Ooh, pardon *moo!* I just love this juicy green grass. So fresh and green. Mmmmmm, so mooo-licious!! *Phhhwwwarrrtttttt!!!* Hmmm, that feels *mooch* better! Moooooo! Now, what's that smell? I can smell something but I can't see it. It couldn't possibly be from *moo-ee*? I wonder where that smell goes? It's amoooozing, really …

Burping and farting cows aren't the only things that contribute to global warming. Pollution from cars, burning coal, aeroplanes, air conditioners, heaters and even old rubbish all play a part too. Although, scientists now believe that the average burping, bottom-rumbling cow can produce the same amount of pollution as a single car! (No wonder nobody has ever taken to driving a cow!)

MOO MOO
POO POO FACTS

- A single cow produces between 100 to 200 litres of methane a day.

- Methane is around 23 times more effective at trapping heat in the Earth's atmosphere than carbon dioxide.

- There are an estimated 1.5 BILLION cows in the world.

- India has the most cows in the world – an estimated 281 million!

- Australia has almost 30 million cows.

- If you feed cows clover and alfalfa instead of grain, it can reduce the methane in their burps and farts by around 25 per cent.

- Cows spend up to eight hours of their day eating.

- Cows often regurgitate their food (bring it back into their mouths) to chew it again. This is called 'chewing the cud' and it helps with their digestion.

MOO MOO POO POO TRIVIA

Apparently, a group of American scientists are working on a way to convert the methane from cow burps and farts into useable power! They have invented a device which traps the methane coming out of a cow's mouth and bottom and stores it in giant gas cylinders. The methane can then be used to power machinery such as tractors. (Now that's what I call Moo Moo Poo Poo Power!)

TOP 10 CATTLE COUNTRIES

REGION   CATTLE POPULATION

India
281,700,000 cows

Brazil
187,087,000 cows

China
139,721,000 cows

USA
96,669,000 cows

Europe
87,650,000 cows

Argentina
51,062,000 cows

Australia
29,202,000 cows

Mexico
26,489,000 cows

South Africa
14,187,000 cows

Key

= 10 million cows

MOO MOO HOO HOOs
Cow jokes!

Q: Why does a milking stool have only three legs?

A: *Because the cow has the udder!*

Q: Why don't cows have any money?

A: *Because the farmers milk them dry.*

Q: What do you call a grumpy cow?

A: *Moo-dy!*

Q: Where do cows like to live?

A: *Moo Zealand, Moo-rocco, and the Moo-n!*

Q: What did the bull say to the cow?

A: *I'm very attracted to moo!*

MOO-ETRY

Little Birdie

ANONYMOUS

Little birdie flying high

Drops a message from the sky

Angry farmer wipes his eye

'Jolly good job cows don't fly!'

FISHY FARTINGS
Sea creatures that blow bottom bubbles

As we know, any animal that has a stomach and intestines (or 'guts') can fart. So, of course, fish and other marine creatures with guts have the ability to do ... fishy farts!

But fishy farts are different from human farts. Human farts come from swallowed air and gases created in the intestines after eating. And they 'pop out' through the rear end only! (Otherwise, it's just a burp!) For most fish, the gases created after they eat just combine with their poo. So fish poo is the only thing that pops out their rear ends! (*Fish poo – eeeeewwwwww!!!*)

However, there are some kinds of fish (like the sand tiger shark) that do blow bubbles out of their rear ends. Blowing out these bubbles (which are mostly made up of air) helps the fish stay at a certain level under water.

And then there's the herring. Not only does the herring blow bubbles out of its fishy bottom, but scientists have recorded a farting sound while it does it! One scientist said it sounded just like a high-pitched raspberry! Scientists believe the farting sound is a way for herring to communicate with each other. (Hello, herring friend? *Phhhwwwwarrrrrttttttt!* Are you out there?? *Phhhwwwarrrrtttttt!!*)

WHALE TAIL EXPLOSIONS
Farting minke!

Have you ever wondered what a whale fart looks like? Well, you don't have to wonder any more … There's a photo!

Some scientists got a stinky surprise one day when they were studying minke whales in the Antarctic. The scientists had been following a pod of whales in a research ship.

They were lucky (or unlucky!) enough to be close to one minke whale at the exact moment it let rip!!

All the scientists said the smell was EXTREMELY stinky. (Imagine a whale-sized gas explosion – *ewwwww!!!!*) Most ran to get away, but one scientist was brave enough to stay put long enough to get a photo. *Snap!* The whale's butt blast was recorded forever!

FISHY FACT FILE

- A group of jellyfish is called a 'smack'.

- Fish are cold-blooded (which means their body temperature changes when the temperature around them changes).

- A group of fish is called a 'school'.

- A jellyfish has no brain.

- Fish existed even before dinosaurs! Scientists think they have been on Earth for around 450 million years.

- Some fish (like herring) use farting as a way to communicate with each other!

FARTY FUNNIES
Salty sea shanty jokes

Q: What type of whales fly?

A: *Pilot whales!*

Q: Why is it easy to weigh fish?

A: *Because they have scales!*

Q: What do you call a singing fish?

A: *A tune-a-fish!*

FARTS 'N' PHYSICS

FARTS 'N' PHYSICS

Albert Einstein was one of the most famous physicists who ever lived. In his lifetime he developed something called the 'theory of relativity' … and he also (you guessed it!) farted!

So did Sir Isaac Newton, Galileo, Michael Faraday and every other physicist who has ever lived!

Farting and physics go hand in hand (or bottom in bottom … Ha!). That's because farting is not just a bodily function, it's also a process that follows many of the rules of physics, such as …

- **decibel**
- **density**
- **momentum**
- **pressure**
- **speed**

That's right, all of the above are involved in the production (and expulsion!) of a bottom boo boo. (If he'd had the time, I'm sure Einstein would have developed a formula for farting – something related to sub-atomic *stinky* particles and their behavior under extreme pressure, perhaps?!)

A fart is a build-up of gases. As we know, as soon as you eat something, your digestive system starts contracting. These contractions help move the food and swallowed air through your body – from your mouth down to your stomach and then through your intestines. When there is enough gas in your intestines, the pressure builds up and the gas is forced out through the nearest opening (your butt!) … This results in what we call a fart!

So, let's take a look at those physics words again:

Decibel A decibel is a way of measuring sound (or how LOUD something is). Farts can be loud or soft, or make no sound at all (like the SBD, the Silent But Deadly!). Apparently, there was a man in Texas who won a competition for having the **LOUDEST** fart. His fart was measured at 168 decibels, which is almost as loud as the sound of a jackhammer!

Density Density is a word which describes the weight of something compared with its size. Imagine you had two 1-litre drink bottles. If you filled one drink bottle up with water and left the other one full of air, which one would be heavier? The one with water, of course! That's because water has a higher density than air. A fart is a mixture of gases (like air), so it has around the same density as air.

Momentum As the gases in your digestive system move through your intestines they pick up momentum until they finally POP out of your bottom as a fart!

Pressure Fart gases can build up inside our intestines, a bit like air inside a balloon. This creates an increase in pressure. The only way to release the pressure is to … let one rip!!

Speed When a fart leaves your body it is moving at a speed of around 30 centimetres per second (or around 1 kilometre per hour).

F= ART² JOKES

Q: What do you call a man who lets one rip while rolling down a hill?

A: *Moe Mentum*

Q: What is the sharpest thing in the world?

A: *A fart – because it goes through your pants and doesn't leave a hole!*

Q: What did the big fart say to the small fart?

A: *You little stinker!*

Q: If your bottom is a universe, where does the universe end?

A: *The Black Hole!*

Q: What does FART mean in physics terms?

A: *F = Frequency, A = Acceleration,
R = Rotation, T = Time*

FART DRAFTING
Bad wind

Drafting happens when bike riders travel in a tight bunch. The riders behind the first rider get to save energy because there is less wind resistance. In a way, they are getting 'pulled' or 'sucked along' by the first bike rider!

Have you ever noticed that sometimes when you fart the smell seems to follow you around even when you try to move away? (*Stop following meeeee!*) Well, I call that 'fart drafting!'

This has happened to all of us at one time or another. You walk into a room, look around and … *Phhhwwaarrrtttt!!!* You release a butt bomb! But no matter which corner of the room you run to, the gassy eggy smell follows you!

Fart drafting happens because when you move you create something called a 'slipstream' (or 'airstream') behind you. When you let one rip, the gas is pulled along on the slipstream, so it literally follows you like bad wind!

Being indoors, in a lift or in a narrow corridor will increase the chance of fart drafting happening to you. So, if you do happen to let one go in an enclosed space, get ready to run like crazy!

NOTE: Bike drafting is not allowed in most triathlon competitions. If someone is caught doing it, he or she can be disqualified! Luckily the same rules don't apply for farting drafting. If you do happen to let one rip in an enclosed space, just hold your nose and get out of there as soon as you can. Once you get into an open space, the fart smell should spread out and fade away!

Fart drafting
no-go zones

Bus Never fart on the bus, unless you don't mind the smell. Even if you run for the back seat, the smell will follow you!

Car Letting one rip in the car is fraught with danger! Even though it's hard to move in a car (so the fart can't follow you), the smell will hang around in the enclosed space until someone opens a window.

Corridor Corridors are usually long and narrow, so if you let one rip, the gassy smell will move wherever you do!

Tunnel Like corridors, tunnels are mostly long and narrow. They are also underground, so there is even less chance for any fart smells to spread out and fade away. The verdict? Never fart in a tunnel (unless you are being chased by your enemies and you want to stink them out!).

Train There are lots of narrow spaces on trains, so it's best not to let one rip unless your train is coming to a stop and you are standing near the doors!

Lift Never, ever fart in a lift. No matter where you move, the fart smell will go with you. If you do have to let one fly, wait until you have reached the floor where you want to get out and run like the wind!

Fart drafting safe zones

Supermarket Supermarkets are full of narrow aisles (which we know are Fart Drafting No-Go Zones!) but with so many people and smells around (roast chickens, cheese, veggies), you are fairly safe to let one fly!

Bank Why not *deposit* some gas in the bank? (Ha!) It can be risky to fart in a bank, but there are usually lots of people around and it should be well ventilated. And it might be the only freebie the bank customers ever get!

A Queue Queues are usually safe places to let fly (as long as the queue is more than three people in length!). It's even better if the queue is moving because you can leave any gassy smells behind. No blame, no shame!

The Great Outdoors The great outdoors is the perfect place to let your butt bubbles be free! After all, it's nature! And with all those wide open spaces, there is little chance that any stinky smells will follow you. Once the butt gas is released, it will spread out and fade away … taking any bad smells with it!

Sport Most sports are played outdoors, so it's safe to let rip! Farting can be a good way to let out any pre-game nerves (like before your soccer grand final!). There are also sports that encourage the release of internal gases, like yoga (it's all that bending and stretching!) and bungy jumping (*Boooiiiiinnng … Phhwwwwaaarrrrtttttttt!!!!!!*).

FARTY POEM

Roses Are Red ...

A. JONES

Roses are red

Violets are blue

Frequently released gas

Makes you go ... ewwwwwwwwwwwww!!!

FARTY FOODS

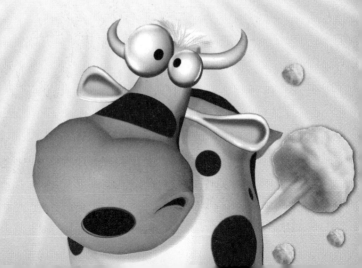

À LA CARTE FART
How to make bigger better bottom bombs

This is the chapter you have all been waiting for … The Butt Blasters Guide on How to Make Bigger Better Bottom Bombs!

Most experienced farters know which foods make their farts more stinky and obnoxious. They go out of their way to eat these foods at any opportunity!

On the next page is a list of 'The Seven Deadly Stinkers'. These are foods that make you produce smelly farts or loud farts – or both! The list has been collected from people of all ages. I've also included a few of my own favourite gastronomic gas makers!

Why not see if you can get your mum or dad to cook one of the Seven Deadly Stinkers for dinner tonight? Eat up, then … BOMBS AWAY!!!

THE SEVEN DEADLY STINKERS!

1 Beans

Beans are nicknamed the 'musical fruit'! That's because beans are famous for causing butt blow-offs!! Beans are part of the legume family (so are lentils, peas, peanuts, soybeans and chickpeas!). Beans contain sugar molecules that humans find hard to digest. The bacteria in our large intestine help us digest the sugar (thanks, guys!), but this also causes LOTS of gas. Luckily, while bean blow-offs might be loud, they are not that stinky!

(Stink scale = 3, Sonic boom = 9)

2 Cabbage

Phewww-eee!! Cabbage is a well-known stink-maker that is eaten in many countries, especially Germany and Russia. It can be eaten in its own (boiled cabbage, anyone??), in soups or stews, or made into coleslaw (yum!). Like broccoli, cabbage is great for you, but it is full of nutrients that are hard to digest. So if you really want to load up on some stinky sulfur-smelling weaponry, reach for the cabbage!

(Stink scale = 7, Sonic boom = 8)

3 Broccoli

Broccoli is part of the cabbage family. It used to be called 'Italian asparagus' because it originally came from Italy! Broccoli is full of Vitamin C and fibre, and it also has lots of things that help to stop you getting cancer. But broccoli also causes TONNES of stinky butt bombs because it's high in sulfate … The two things to remember about broccoli are: it's great fart fuel and it's really good for you! So you can fluff your way to good health!!

(Stink scale = 5, Sonic boom = 8)

4 Eggs

How do you like to eat your eggs? Scrambled, fried, poached, hard boiled, soft boiled or with buttered toast soldiers? Whichever way you eat them, eggs are high in sulfur so they are likely to give you egg-tremely STINKY gas! In fact, eggy farts are so powerful they can stink out an entire room and the smell will linger for hours!

(Stink scale = 9, Sonic boom = 7)

5 Onions

Onions are another fantastic gas-producing weapon! If you only had two weapons in your farty bag of tricks, then onions and beans would be the ones to pick! Whether you eat it raw or cooked, the onion can conjure up magical amounts of gas and smelliness. Every farting machine should have one!!

(Stink scale = 7, Sonic boom = 9)

6 Garlic

Garlic is in the same family as the onion and has been around for over 6,000 years. It is used in lots of tasty dishes, like garlic bread and spaghetti bolognaise. Garlic is also high in sulfur, so it's great for creating some super stinky garlicky butt-bombs!!

(Stink scale = 7, Sonic boom = 5)

7 Lentils

Lentils are a vegetarian's favourite! They are full of healthy stuff like protein, fibre and Vitamin B. But lentils are also one of those foods that are hard for humans to digest, so they cause plenty of windy pops! In fact, if you cooked up some lentil soup with onions, you would probably create enough gas for a LENTIL LIFT-OFF! They are great for sonic boom sound-effects too!
(Stink scale = 3, Sonic boom = 10!!)

Other farty foods

Foods like apples, asparagus, bread, corn, fizzy drinks, prunes, milk and even diet lollies can also cause windy pops. But nothing beats the Seven Deadly Stinkers for creating really eye-poppingly stinky (and NOISY) butt blow-offs!!

Farty Tip #4: If you cook cabbage for around six minutes and eat it, you are likely to produce DOUBLE the amount of butt blow-offs than if you cooked it for only three minutes!!!

TWELVE DASTARDLY DEADLY DISHES!

Some dishes are better than others when it comes to producing jumbo-sized butt bombs! Ask your parents to prepare one of the deadly dishes below for lunch or dinner … and then let the farty family fun begin!

1 Lentil soup

Lentil soup is full of nutrients. It's also full of fibre which makes your backside go POP!! But feel free to eat up – lentil farts aren't that smelly!!

2 French onion soup

Another soupy, farty delight! French onion soup is a traditional dish of France. The French love it, but I wonder if they like the farty aftershocks? (Ha!)

3 Steamed fish and broccoli

A healthy dish that will have you farting in no time!
Make sure you don't eat this on a first date – broccoli butt
bombs are SMELLY! (*Pheeeew!*)

4 Baked beans on toast

A butt bomb classic! This dish is guaranteed to have you
tootin' out some botty tunes before dessert!

5 Three bean salad

The three bean salad is what I like to call a 'triple threat dish'! There's *three times* the farting power in this little beauty!! If you are eating a three bean salad, you are probably on a picnic in the great outdoors, so eat up – and then feel part of (stinky) nature!!

6 Egg and lettuce sandwich

Yum! One of the best sandwich combinations around. It's also one of the best sandwiches for producing big eggy farts! (*Ewwww!!!*)

7 Milkshake

Dairy products are delicious – and they also cause flatulence! Choose your flavour (chocolate, strawberry, honeycomb, lime) and make sure you drink through a straw (it makes you swallow more air!) for a milkshake-POPPING good time! Don't forget to slurp up the last little bits for a satisfying butt bang finale!

8 Corned beef with cauliflower in white sauce

Mmmm ... Salty corned beef and cheesy cauliflower. Guaranteed to cause a bottom-burp concert after eating. In fact, some people think corned beef makes their farts smell like seaweed! (Weird!!)

9 Cold potato salad

Potato salad is made from potatoes that have been cooked and then left to go cold. Eating potatoes this way creates more gas than eating hot potatoes. So tuck in and then ... LET RIIIIIIIP!!!

10 Fried tomatoes and onions

This dish will make you burp *and* fart! Tomatoes are known for making people burp while onions are great fuel for rocket-powered *butt* burps!

11 Stewed apples and prunes

An apple a day keeps the doctor away ... unless you're the fart doctor! Add some prunes for even more butt-blasting impact!!

12 Sausages with fried cabbage

Sausages cause lots of gas. So does cabbage! Eat these foods together to create truly earth-shattering BOTTOM BOMBS!

FARTY FOOD FUNNIES

Q: What kind of fruit farts?

A: *A raspberry!*

Q: What do you get if you eat onions
and baked beans?

A: *Tear gas*
*(Ha! Get it? Because cutting up onions makes you cry
and baked beans make you gassy?!)*

Q: What do you call a nasty legume?

A: *A mean bean!*

FARTY POEM

Beans, Beans ...

ANONYMOUS

Beans, beans are good for your heart

The more you eat, the more you fart

The more you fart, the better you feel

So let's have beans with every meal!

FART -ERCISE

FARTY SPORTS
Popping good exercises!

Have you ever noticed that when you are playing sport you are more likely to *pop off* than at other times? Well, this is your body's natural reaction to all that jumping and moving around – after all, there's nothing more natural than farting!

If you feel like it's time to let your gas be free, try my Top 7 Gassy Sports and Exercises below!

1 Weightlifting

Weightlifting is an Olympic sport. It's also good for Olympic-sized farts!! In Olympic weightlifting, contestants have to lift a bar with heavy weights above their heads. This involves a lot of grunting and straining. Your insides will strain too, increasing the chance of pushing out a butt bomb. The good news is that you can always grunt loudly to cover up any farting sounds!!

Best tip to hide farting: Grunt at the exact same time you let one rip!

2 Yoga

Yoga is a form of gentle exercise and relaxation … and it's famous for causing butt blow-offs! Apparently yoga twists and stirs up your guts – and your gut gas! You know what it's like – you're in a yoga class quietly minding your own business and then … *Phhhhhwwwwaarrrp!!!* The person next to you blasts away on their butt trumpet! It's very distracting. But then … *Phhhhhwwwwaarrrp!!!* This time it's you! You can't help it – yoga just has that effect on people!

Best farty yoga pose: The downward dog

3 Football

Football is a fun game to play with your mates. But sometimes when your leg lets fly to kick the ball, something else lets fly too! Butt bombs are pretty common in footy. But with all the running and shouting (not to mention sweaty players!), no one really notices. A butt bomb or two may even be helpful in throwing off your opposition!

Best sport for secret farting: Footy!

4 Gymnastics

Running, tumbling, back flips, forward rolls, handstands and twirls are all part of gymnastics … and so is farting! Gymnasts put a lot of effort into their routines, so it's no surprise that sometimes a little extra GAS pops out!! If it happens during a competition, just smile and keep going … the judges might even score you extra marks for it!

Best gymnastics tip: If your best friend tells you she had cabbage soup for dinner, don't offer to spot her during a handstand – unless you want a face full of fart gas!!!

5 Running

Running helps you stay fit and healthy – and it also helps your digestion. While you are running, the gas in your system moves along at great speed ... until it POPS out through your bottom! Running farts are usually small but frequent – some people do a little bottom burp every six or seven strides. Running is often the best time to play your butt trumpet because you won't smell it ... (too bad about the person running behind you!!).

Best time to fart: When you are running long distance – you will leave the smell far behind!

6 Bowling

The aim of ten-pin bowling is to knock down the pins at the end of your lane. You pick up a bowling ball, put your fingers in the holes, throw your arm back and … *baaaarrrrppp!* Your butt trumpet blasts while the ball goes rolling down the lane! (Hey, if you knock down all ten pins in bowling it's called a strike. Does that mean if you knock down all ten pins *and* you let one rip, it's called a butt strike??)

Best farty advice: Let one rip at the exact moment you release the bowling ball – it might give you extra power!

7 Wrestling

Whether it's a wrestling competition or you are just mucking around with your brother on the floor, wrestling gets your gut gas popping!! Like yoga, wrestling stretches and massages your internal organs. All this movement makes the gas travel more quickly through your digestive system. Your wrestling partner might also grab you around the middle which can cause some gas to accidentally POP out!

Best wrestling tip: Don't challenge your brother to a wrestling match straight after he's eaten an entire can of baked beans!!

DARE TO FART

FART DARES
When farts attack!

WARNING: This chapter should be used with extreme caution! Only try the following dares when you are in a situation where a little humour is called for … or when you are feeling really, really naughty!!!!!!

Farts have been used as a weapon for as long as there have been people farting. (Just think about the games you play with your brothers or sisters!) So the time has come for me to share with you my favourite …

Top 5 Fart Attack Dares!

1 The Lift Leftover

This one is particularly sneaky because everyone is trapped in a small, confined space. Get a butt blast ready, then hop into the nearest lift. (It's best if the lift is going up, because hot air rises!) Stand right at the front, as if you are about to get out on the next floor. Then, just before the doors open, unleash your babbling bottom blockbuster … As the doors open, a slight gust of wind will waft in and spread your smelly offering right through the lift! (If you are feeling brave enough, turn around, give a little wave and call out 'Enjoy!' to the people inside as the doors close!)

2 The Car Corker

This dare has a no-escape clause! That means that once you release your gassy load, you have to sit there and suck it up with the rest of the passengers. If you are brave enough to try it, make sure you are in a car with five passengers and the windows rolled up. Wait until the car is just about to take off from the lights, then … LET RIP! (The movement of the car will help disguise the thunder from down under!) Afterwards, you can either stare out the window and act oblivious while the other passengers' nostrils burn … Or, you can turn to the person next to you and say, 'Good one! *Phewwwwwww!* That stinks! Good on ya!!'

3 The Bus Banger

A bus is a great place to carry out a fart attack dare. Try to stand near a group of people so you have an audience who can enjoy (or endure!) your passing moment. Wait until the bus is just about to stop, then let one rip! When the doors open, a gust of wind will disperse your gassy scent throughout the bus ... to be enjoyed by all of the fare-paying passengers! (Nice!)

4 The Party Farty

It's great to celebrate at a get-together with your mates or family members. Whether it's a birthday party, Christmas dinner, New Year's Eve or even a school disco! Pick your moment well – wait until everyone is up on their feet and a speech is being made. Make sure you are right up the front where the speech-maker is standing. Get one primed and ready for launch … As soon as the speech ends and people start clapping, BOMBS AWAY!! (It gives new meaning to the term 'party pooper'!)

5 The Scuddle Huddle

This little ripper is an absolute no-brainer at a sporting event! Whether you play soccer, netball, rugby league, AFL or any other sport where you get to hug your fellow players, this should work like poetry in motion. As soon as your team goes into a huddle and you have your arms around the players next to you, load up a ripe raspberry. When the huddle is ready to break, say, 'Hang on, everyone … one more thing!' then POP it out. (And then run like crazy!!!! Guaranteed to get a laugh!)

FARTY TRIVIA
Farty balloons

Did you know that in a single day, you might produce around 2.5 litres of fart gas?! That's about the same amount of gas it takes to fill up a party balloon!!

FARTY POEM

Super Dooper Potty Pooper

A. JONES

Super dooper potty pooper

I can't find my pooper scooper

I will have a saggy nappy

If I don't get to the toilet … snappy!

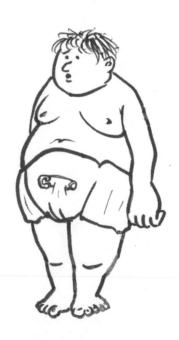

FARTITUDE

FARTITUDE
High-altitude flatus explosions

Do you fart more if you are standing on top of a mountain (which is called high altitude)? Or standing on the flat ground below (which is called sea level)??

When you're at high altitudes (for example, standing on a mountain top or flying in a plane), the air pressure is lower than when you're standing on the ground. But what does that mean?

Well, when you think of air, you probably think of emptiness or nothingness. (*Are you there, air??*) But air is actually *pushing* on everything, all the time!

When you're at high altitudes, the air around you is pushing on your body less than it does when you're standing on flat ground. This can make the gas in your stomach *expand*. (It gives new meaning to the words 'bulging waistline', doesn't it?!)

If you are hiking up a mountain or flying in a plane, you may feel a tightness in your stomach as the gas inside it expands. This can lead to an increase in the amount of windy pops you do, as your body tries to let the gas be free!

During World War II, doctors discovered that at heights above 30,000 feet, some pilots suffered from swollen tummies because of the expanding gas in their intestines. As the outside air pressure went down, the volume occupied by the gas in their stomachs went up. (See, farting *is* science – not just pop and crackle!)

It's also well known among skydivers that when a plane gets to around 6,000 feet, you are more likely to hear some sky-high BUTT BANGS! (I wonder if *fear* causes a few windy pops as well?!)

FARTY TRIVIA
Fart signals

The human body is very clever. It knows how to send signals when there's too much gas building up inside of you. One of the signals is a stomach ache. When you have swallowed too much air (or eaten lots of gas-producing foods, like broccoli), the excess gas can cause your stomach to *streeeeeetch*. Ouch! The pain usually goes away as soon as you burp or fart and your stomach returns to its normal size. (But if it doesn't, make sure you tell your mum or dad!)

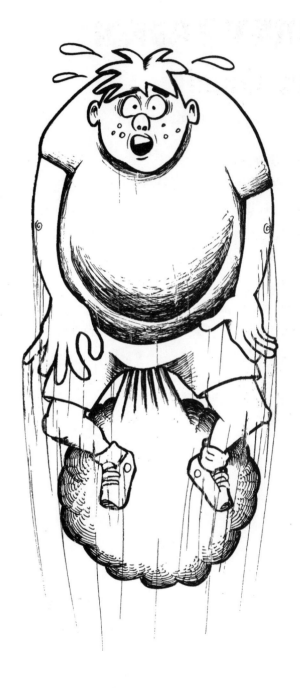

FARTY FUNNY

Q: What do you call a fart at sea level?

A: *Flat-u-lence!*
(Hahahaha! Get it? Because sea level is flat?!)

FARTS
IN
SPACE

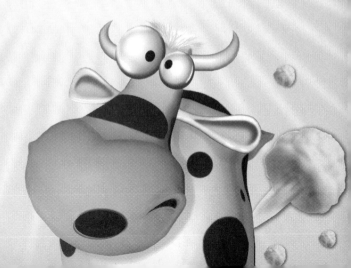

FARTS IN SPACE
Intergalactic farts

Have you ever stared up at the sky at night? Space seems so big, wide and endless … When we think of space, we think of bright stars, orbiting planets, supernovas and even black holes!

But what do space and farting have in common?? Well, some people say that the creation of the universe was caused by something called The Big Bang. But other people like to call this The Great Galactic Fart!!!

THE BIG BANG

Human beings have always been fascinated by space. In the 1950s and '60s, Russia and America were in a competition to see which country would be the first to put a man on the Moon. This was called the 'Space Race'. (Some people think the race was actually about being the first man ever to *fart* in space ... but this has not been proven!) In 1969, America won the race when US astronaut Neil Armstrong was the first man ever to take a step on the Moon.

But before Neil Armstrong could get to the Moon, lots of things had to be researched by scientists. One of these things was whether an astronaut farting in space would be DANGEROUS. The scientists were worried a fart might actually cause a fire or explosion onboard a space shuttle! (Talk about *explosive* butt bombs!!)

The scientists eventually decided that farting in space wouldn't cause a fire. But for many years, they still banned astronauts from eating 'gassy' foods like broccoli and cabbage ... just to be on the safe side!

Cosmic farting power

A few years ago, an American astronaut decided to do his own farty experiment while up in space. He tried to propel himself forward using nothing but his own FART POWER! The astronaut thought that he was 'blessed' with extraordinary natural farting abilities. But although he pushed out a MASSIVE butt bomb with great speed, unfortunately he failed to move very far … Maybe he just needed to push out a few butt bombs in a row?!

FARTY SPACE FACTS
True or false?

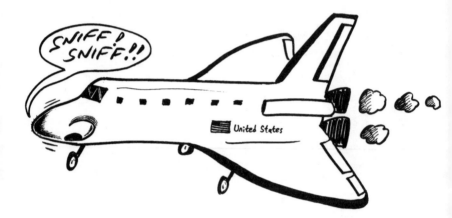

FSF1 – Scientists have developed something called an Electronic Nose (or ENose) to sniff out harmful gases on space shuttles.

TRUE! The ENose is a device that can recognise almost any smell. (It's like an extremely advanced version of a smoke detector!) An ENose can even tell the difference between Coke and Pepsi! It works a bit like a human nose, but it's much more sensitive. The device is about the size of a shoebox and has 32 'sensors' that help it detect different smells. An ENose is helpful to astronauts because it can sniff out tiny amounts of dangerous gases.

(I wonder if that includes excess fart gas?!) They are also used by scientists on Earth. Imagine how handy it would be if you had an ENose in your house – it could warn you the second your sister dropped an SBD (Silent But Deadly)!!!

FSF2 – **Scientists have developed an engine that is powered by fart gas!**

TRUE! Sort of … Most rocket engines are powered by liquid oxygen and hydrogen or solid chemicals. But in 2007, scientists tested an engine that was powered by liquid methane! Now, we know that methane is one of the gases that is often found in human farts. Methane can also be found on Mars, Jupiter and many other planets, so it would be a handy space fuel. When scientists tested the liquid methane, it made a dazzling blue flame blast out of the engine. (I wonder if that's the equivalent of a rocket fart?!)

FSF3 – **If an astronaut farted while floating in space, they could open a flap in their space suit to let the smell out.**

FALSE! If an astronaut is floating in space, their specially designed space suit is the only thing that gives them oxygen and protects them from the atmosphere outside. Outer space is pretty dangerous! If an astronaut got a large tear in their space suit, they would be in BIG trouble! Firstly, they would fall unconscious in about 15 seconds because there's no oxygen. Then their blood would start to boil because there's no air pressure. This would make their heart, liver and skin start to swell up. By now they would probably freeze because temperatures in space can get as low as -100°C in the shade. Finally, they would be zapped by radiation (like cosmic rays) and hit by high-speed space dust and rocks. *Ouch!!* So if an astronaut farts in space, he or she just has to suck it up (literally!) and wait till they get back to the space shuttle to get some fresh air!

ARRRGH!!!

SPACE FUNNIES

Q: When do astronauts have lunch?

A: *Launch time!!*

Q: What kind of saddle does a space cowboy use?

A: *A saddle-lite!*

Q: What do you call a crazy moon?

A: *A luna-tic!*

Q: How does the solar system hold up its pants?

A: *With an asteroid belt!*

Q: What does the *Star Wars* character Yoda and a fart have in common?

A: *They both have 'odour' in them!*

WORLD WIDE FARTS

FARTIONALITY
The international fart

Throughout history, English-speaking people have always made up funny names for farting. The good news is that just about every other culture on the planet has done their bit to make up funny fart names as well! Yes, just like us, they have serious and seriously *silly* names for bottom blowing …

Your mission (if you choose to accept it) is to try to remember how to pronounce the word 'fart' in two or more of the languages on the following pages. (My favourite is the Korean word for a windy pop!)

Remember, being able to speak another language is an invaluable tool. It will not only impress other people, it will also open the channels of communication between different cultures … (Hey, you gotta start somewhere!)

NOTE: It's a good idea to learn how to say 'hello' in the languages below (so that you don't start with the word 'fart' when you first meet a person from another country!).

Chinese   *Pi* (pronounced **pee**)

Danish   *Prut* (pronounced **put**)

Dutch   *Scheet* (pronounced **sheet**)

French   *pêt* (pronounced **peh**)

German   *Furz* (pronounced **ferts**)

Hebrew   *Flotz* (pronounced **floats**)

Hungarian   *Fing* (pronounced **feeng**)

Indonesian   *Kentut* (pronounced **ken-toot**)

Italian   *Peto* (pronounced **pet-o**)

Japanese   *Onara* (pronounced **on-air-a**)

Korean   *Pongu* (pronounced **pong-goo**)

Latin   *Bombulum*
(pronounced **bom-bull-oom**)

Lebanese   *Fuss* (pronounced **ferss**)

Persian   *Gooz* (pronounced **guzz**)

Russian   *Puk* (pronounced **pook**)

Spanish   *Pedo* (pronounced **peddo**)

Swedish   *Fiser* (pronounced **fee-sir**)

FARTING CULTURE

Did you know that in many cultures farting is seen as a natural process that is good for your physical, spiritual and mental wellbeing?

The ancient Arabs thought that farting was a way of 'purifying' (or cleansing) your body because it let out the evil spirits! Not only that, it was perfectly okay to fart in front of others. (I'm sure your mum would love that! Imagine if you let one rip at a family dinner in front of all your relatives … 'It's okay, Mum. I'm just purifying!' NOT!!)

The ancient Arabs also had lots of names for farters. Anyone who could produce LOUD pop-offs was called *Eboo-ez-Zirteh* (or The Father of Farts). But people who let off silent-but-stinky farts were called *Fezwaun* (or Fizzler), which was an insult! Finally, anyone who could fluff out a tune without stinking up a storm was called Simojeh-el-Hewweh (or Breaker of Wind). Now wouldn't that make a great Christmas CD?! *Jingle Smells, Jingle Smells …*

The Canelos Indians of Ecuador were said to be scared of their own farts! They had a belief that when you farted, your soul would escape your body. To make sure that the farter's soul didn't completely escape from their body, the person sitting closest to them had to slap them on the back three times. The farter also had to prepare a big feast for everyone. (If we did that in my family, my brother would never stop cooking and I would never stop slapping him on the back!!)

In France, apparently farting is quite acceptable. King Louis XIV of France once let one *riiiip* right in front of his sister-in-law. He told her it was a sign of how much he admired her! (There's someone like King Louis in every family, isn't there?)

But in England, they are more timid about their farts! The Earl of Oxford accidentally farted one time when he was bowing to Queen Elizabeth I. He was so embarrassed, he left England and didn't come back for seven years!!

FARTY FUNNY

Q: What do you call a fart that can't be seen, heard or smelled?

A: *A gas ghost!*

FARTY TRIVIA
Warm wind

As we know, humans make wind! But there are also warm winds that occur in nature. One of the most famous warm winds is called Sirocco. The Sirocco starts in the Sahara desert and picks up moisture as it moves over the Mediterranean Sea. By the time it reaches Italy, the wind is warm and humid, which is why it is known as the GREAT ITALIAN FART!

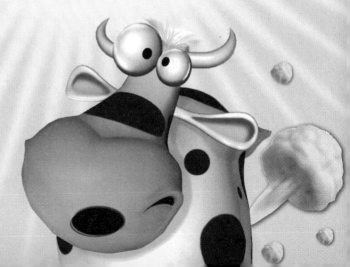

FART
IN
ART

FART ARTISTS

Mr Methane and Le Pétomane are two famous fart artists. But you can be a fart artist too! Turn the page for some tips on designing and drawing your own fart masterpieces. Make sure you label your drawing so you get the credit!

Now, Ready Steady … FART!!

Top 10 Fart Masterpieces (FMs)

FM1   Design a type of transport that is powered by fart gas.

FM2   Draw a fart that might be used to help someone get out of a tricky situation.

FM3   Draw an electric-powered fart.

FM4   Design a fart machine that might help people in their daily lives.

FM5   Draw a fart tattoo design.

FM6   Draw some of your own farts! (Use your imagination to work out what they might look like.)

FM7   Design a futuristic fart machine that might help power a planet.

FM8   Design a new invention that uses fart power in some way.

FM9   Draw an invisible fart.

FM10   Draw a fart masterpiece. This can be anything you want it to be … (as long as it's GASSY! Ha!)

NOTE: Your fart masterpieces can incorporate anything at all that is related to farting. They can include people, places, funny situations or events. You can draw and create new inventions that are powered by methane gas, butt bubbles, raspy raspberries, roaring rippers, botty bombs … or any type of fart-related sound or subject!

FARTIVITIES
Fart Activities (FAs)

Below are some fun activities to keep you busy on a rainy (or windy!) day. Guaranteed to beat the boredom blues with hours of farting fun!

FA1   Try to name every single one of your farts (for example, The Happy, The Squeaker …).

FA2   Try to identify what you have eaten by smelling your own fart gas. (*Ewwwww! Curried egg sandwich!!*)

FA3   Count how many farts you do in one hour. (*Number 6, Number 7, Number 8 …*)

FA4   Write down what time you do the loudest and the softest farts.

FA5   Grab a stopwatch and time how long one of your farts lasts. (You might need a friend to help you with this one!)

FA6 Fart in a few different rooms in your house. Try to work out if the farts are louder in one particular room (for example, the bathroom).

FA7 Do a fart standing up and then lying down. Take note of which fart is louder and which fart lasts longer.

FARTY POEM

Farts Are …

A. JONES

Farts are …

> *loud*
> > *squeaky*
> > > *smelly*
> > > > *and sneaky!*

Farts are …

> *tight*
> > *loose*
> > > *wide*
> > > > *and obtuse!*

Farts can …

> *rip*
> > *roar*
> > > *blast*
> > > > *and bore!*

Farts can …

> sing
>> shout
>>> hurt
>>>> and blow out!

Farts can …

> bark
>> ruff
>>> bang
>>>> and bluff!

Farts can …

> croak
>> toot
>>> yodel
>>>> and poot!

JOBS THAT MAKE YOU GO BOOOOM!!

TOP 5 FARTY PROFESSIONS

Some jobs seem to be a little more gassy than others!
I have done a bit of fart detective work (including
interviews, spying and lie-detector tests!) to find out
the Top 5 Farty Professions …

1 Teacher

Have you ever seen your teacher standing up the front of
the class, explaining something to the students, when in
mid-sentence they suddenly stop and give a half-smile that
turns into a smirk? Well, it's likely you have been a witness
to an SBD (Silent But Deadly). You might have noticed a
pungent eggy smell and thought to yourself, *'Hmmm, it
wasn't me … or any of the students next to me. In fact, the
only person close enough to attack my nostrils with goo goo
gas is … NO WAY! … the teacher!!!'* As unbelievable as it
may seem, your teacher will sneak out the odd raspberry
in class. Teachers are only human, and when the gas gods
rumble in their tummies it's time to stand back because
their internal eggnog is about to explode …

Check out the following **Farting By Profession Tips (FBPTs!)**:

FBPT1 If your teacher is talking to the class and starts to smirk mid-sentence, get ready to cover your nose!

FBPT2 If your teacher is standing at the front of the class and suddenly moves quickly in another direction, beware! (It's likely your teacher has dropped a BOMB and is fleeing the scene of the crime!)

FBPT3 If your teacher tells you they had broccoli soup for dinner, don't follow them up the stairs – always walk in front!

2 Yoga/Pilates Instructor

Yoga and Pilates are groups of exercises that make your body strong and flexible. Many people believe these exercises 'massage' your internal organs. All that bending and stretching is also famous for producing bottom blasts! If you are a yoga or Pilates instructor, this will happen to you more often than most … Yes, there's nothing like twisting your body into a classic yoga position and then unleashing a core butt blast that has been hiding deep within the recesses of your tummy! (Turn the page for the best yoga positions for producing breathtaking bottom burps.)

FBPT1 If you feel a little windy before yoga, always sit at the very back of the class so that when you release a bottom belch no one will know exactly where it came from!

FBPT2 To decrease the chance of windy pops, never eat or chew gum right before a yoga class.

FBPT3 If you do happen to release an explosion during class, just laugh and say, 'Ha! I shouldn't have had that banana pineapple low-fat skim-milk smoothie for lunch!' This will make your fellow yoga classmates nod understandingly … (even if they all know you really had a burger!)

Top 7 Farty Yoga Positions

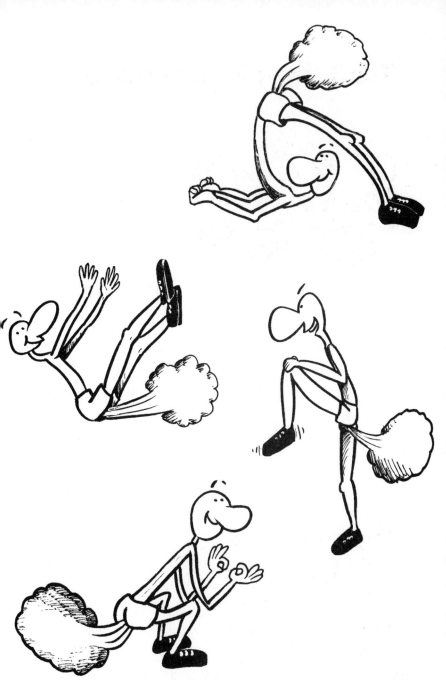

The Master!

3 Doctor

Every doctor has uttered the famous phrase: *'Don't worry. I've seen it all before. I'm a doctor …'* Well, this might be true, but doctors are human as well. Just like you and me, they eat, sleep and, of course … FART! Yes, that's right, doctors let rip and probably more than most because they know the health benefits of releasing gaseous waste into the world. In a doctor's surgery there are many smelly things: antiseptic, rubber gloves, jelly beans (yum), needles and medicines. A doctor can safely let one rip while they are examining you because they know the smell will probably blend in with the surrounding odours. If it doesn't, they will just tell you that it's healthy to expel gas! And who can argue with doctor's orders?!

FBPT1 If your doctor lets one rip, say nothing, just keep on chatting. The act of farting has become so natural to them that they won't even notice – and they won't expect you to notice, either!

FBPT2 If your doctor is examining you and you let one rip while he or she is prodding and poking your belly, just smile and say nothing. Your doctor will act like they didn't hear or smell a thing … they might just ask you if you have been eating lots of fibre!

FBPT3 If you are sitting in a doctor's waiting room, there will probably be a lot of people around so it is perfectly acceptable to unleash a ripe raisin bottom bomb! If anyone notices, just say you are seeing the doctor because you have a tummy upset!

4 Taxi Driver

Being a taxi driver can be a stressful job! Not only do you have to navigate traffic all day, you have to deal with every type of personality that jumps into your taxi. The air in a taxi is often a curious mix of perfume, body odour, food, petrol fumes and of course … farts!!! Taxis collect the smells of all who enter. These smells can linger like low-level gas clouds, penetrating even the most tightly clenched nostrils. Plus, taxi drivers sometimes work for 12 hours a day. They have to grab whatever food they can – fruit, sandwiches, burgers, chips, lollies and soft drinks. This is like a perfect fart recipe – lots of different foods and then lots of time for the gas to ferment in the intestines … It's no wonder many taxi drivers boast that they have come close to developing the best GAS BOMBS known to mankind!!

FBPT1 Never sit up the front with the taxi driver. This is a 'No-Go Gas Zone' – anything can happen up there!

FBPT1 If you are squashed in the back seat of a taxi with other people, it's okay to let out a bottom burp or two – just try to make sure they are not too smelly!

5 Politician

This profession deserves a special mention. People usually become politicians because they love to talk. And talk and talk and talk … In fact, many politicians seem to have been born with a special ability to open their mouths and talk about any topic for hours and hours. This makes some people say that politicians are full of 'hot wind' and that they love 'gasbagging'. Other people say that politicians never stop blowing their own trumpets. (I wonder if that means their butt trumpets as well?!)

FBPT1 Never stand directly in front of a politician when they are gasbagging – the amount of hot air coming out might make you feel dizzy!

FBPT2 If a politician suddenly stops talking, beware … It may be that the hot wind is about to come from another direction!

Notable Farty Professions

The following farty professions didn't make it into our Top 5, but they are still worth a mention!

Dentist Many dentists have a wicked sense of humour. While you are trapped in the dentist chair with bits of equipment in your mouth, they will relish the opportunity to let out a tooth-rattling, jaw-dropping, nostril-smacking stinker! Evil!!!

Greengrocer Greengrocers are soooo healthy! They have unlimited access to all those delicious fruits and veggies. But while fruit and veggies are nature's wonder foods, they are also well-known for making you GASSY! That's right, a greengrocer can fart with the best of them. They produce the freshest, organically grown bean bombs all year round … but watch out if it's cabbage season!!

Accountant Accountants like to count their farts and keep bottom-burp receipts, just in case they are ever asked to produce a record of their annual farts. Many also like to eat comfort food (like burgers, chips and soft drinks) to help them produce tax-deductible farts!

Chef Food glorious food … Chefs love to cook and they love to eat! A chef gets to nibble and taste everything they cook, all day long. The rumour is that chefs can create the most bombastic, belly-churning bottom burps in the world. True *à la carte* farts!!!

POPPING PERSONALITIES

FARTY PERSONALITY TYPES
Which farter are you?

There are lots of different types of farters in the world. See if you can identify yourself from the species below!

The Animal Farts anywhere, anytime, in front of anyone! This fluffer is loud and proud!

The Athlete Someone who likes to fart BIG, then sprints into the distance like a thief in the night!

The Copy Cat This person is always ready to let a fart fizz as soon as someone else has just dropped a bomb!

The Farteologist Like an archeologist, this person has the ability to dig up a fart from somewhere deep in their digestive system that has been trapped for years and years – and smells like it as well!!

The Fibber This person drops really toxic smelly gas bombs and always blames someone else. (Remember, the blamer is nearly always the maker!)

The Fool Likes to drop a butt belch and then break into hysterical laughter. (Then drops another and another … And another!)

The Genius Knows how to time a fart exactly when they are leaving somewhere so the blame can't be assigned to him or her!

The Legend Raises his or her leg before belting out a bionic butt blast. This person thinks that everyone waits on his or her next explosion like it's Christmas!

The Rodent Like a mouse, this person just lets out little squeaks here and there. (They need to eat more fibre!!)

The Romantic This person farts and then gets all teary eyed because the bottom burp just left home!

The Sneak The master of the SBD (Silent But Deadly) fart! This person has the ability to ease out a fart with the stealth of a B2 bomber, which means they have incredible (stinky!) accuracy and usually manage to go undetected!

The Witch Can conjure up an evil-smelling concoction in the blink of an eye (or should that be in the blink of a *toad's* eye??)

FART SPECIES

Farts come in all different sizes and sounds! Check out the Fart Species below to see if you can identify your own botty bangers (and those of your family!).

The Baked Bean Bang A series of loud pop-offs that sound like someone's banging on a set of tympani drums!

The Bullet One very quick and loud *PLOOF!*

The Buzzer Sounds like a buzzer on a game show!

The Cough Croak It sounds like a frog's croak and pops out at the same time as you cough!

The Chainsaw Sounds like a chainsaw cutting wood – it makes your butt cheeks vibrate too!

The Egg Bomb Stinks like rotten eggs!

The Faa! Makes the same noise as when you bite your bottom lip and then *flick* it out!

The Fa-fa-fa-fa Sounds like a helicopter coming in to land.

The Faker Someone who puts his or her hand under their arm and makes a fart noise.

The Fluffy Fizzer Sounds like air coming out of a bike tyre or a very small gas leak – Mum's favourite! (Ha!)

The Ghost Can't be seen or heard … but it can be smelt!

The Onion Rip Sounds like ripping paper.

The Rump Rumbler A loud and explosive fart that can last for up to 15 seconds!!

The Silent But Deadly (The SBD) A fart that slips out silently so no one realises you have done it … until it stinks up the entire room!

The Sneeze Squeeze Explodes out when you sneeze – usually with a big bang!

The Squeaker Sounds like a tiny mouse squeak.

The Thunder Thud The biggest of the lot! This beastly butt bang rattles doors and windows and scares small animals close by!

THE BLAME GAME (Who me? No way!)

Now that you know what type of farter you are (and the types of farts you do!), you can play 'the blame game'. Below are the Top 10 ways to get out of stinky situations!

1 The Slinky Stinky Sidestep

If you are standing with a group of people and you let one slip, just sloooowly sidestep away from the crowd … If you can, look at another person and roll your eyes, as if acknowledging the fact that 'someone' has dropped a bomb and scooted!

2 The Antique Furniture Fluff

If you are sitting on an antique chair or lounge, you can release a butt bomb and blame it on the furniture. *'Did you hear that? This seat is so squeaky! Maybe it's broken!'* Move around on the seat to really make it squeak and squawk. This will draw attention to the noise while your stinky gut gas fades away!

3 The Exclamation Fart

If you let one rip and you're standing in a small group, the best diversion is the old 'OMG!! Who did that?! That's horrible! Woah, that really PONGS!' You will divert attention away from yourself (but you have to have the persuasion skills of a used car salesman to *really* get away with this one!).

4 The Golden Oldie

If your grandparents are visiting and you release a big banger, just throw a meaningful look in your granny or pop's direction. Everyone will think that it was them and not you! (Don't worry, your grandparents won't mind … they probably did the same thing to their grandparents!)

5 Blame it on Billy

If you are at a family get-together and you accidentally do a windy pop, blame the little kids! This always works well because little kids usually overreact. You could say something like, 'Whoaaaaaaaa … Billy, you little grommet. Phewwww!! That stinks!' Billy will protest and say it wasn't him. Just shake your head and say, 'Yeah, right …'

6 The 'I heard nothing ...'

If you drop a really LOUD butt bomb, just ignore it and keep doing what you were doing. Say nothing at all! If someone says, 'Did you hear that?' Just say, 'Hear what??'

7 The Storm Brewer

If you let one rip and it's really really LOUD, look up at the sky in a puzzled way. Turn to the person next to you and say, 'Did you hear that? I think it was thunder. There must be a storm on the way!'

BOOM!
RUMBLE!

8 The Singalong

If you are in a social situation and you just can't hold it in any longer, burst into song! Yes, that's right! Sing and clap your hands as you release your little gas monster. The clapping will disguise the sound and the singing will distract people. Even if the smell attacks their nostrils, they won't know who to blame!

Song suggestions: 'Row, Row, Row Your Boat', 'The Chicken Dance' and 'Ten Green Bottles'.

9 The 'Did you know?'

If one pops out and it takes you by surprise, the best way to divert attention is to make a bizarre comment (like, *'Did you know that you can go fishing on the moon?'*) and then walk away really quickly. The person will be so busy trying to understand your crazy comment that they won't even realise you left some stinky gut gas behind!

10 The Animal Cracker

This is a classic excuse but it works every time! If you accidentally blow your butt trumpet, blame the dog, the cat or even the budgie! Animals will never argue with you and dogs are famous for dropping really smelly tummy truffles (farts!). The bigger the animal, the easier it will be to convince everyone around that it was them and not you! *'Naughty Kitty. No more milk for you!'*

FARTY POEM

What Am I?

A. JONES

I'm invisible and loud but squeak like a mouse

I sneak under doors and into your house

I seep through the cracks and fill up the space

I spread like a blanket all over the place

I waft over here but start over there

I'm silent but deadly, you're never aware

I tickle the hair down deep in your nose

I burrow like air inside of your clothes

I linger around like an unwelcome guest

I come in the daytime and when you're at rest

I can be contagious but cannot be caught

Your brain can make me from one silly thought

I am much more than the sum of my parts

I'm something we all do and that is to … FART!

FAMILY FUMES

FAMILY FUMES
The family that farts together stays together

Now, let's talk about families!

I'm sure every family has at least one member who lets rip with more power, projection and pungency than any other person in the family. This phenomenon is known as **EHFF - Extra High Farting Frequency!!**

Some scientists think that farting runs in families, just like hair colour or eye colour! That means that some families might be more 'farty' than others. There are a few reasons for this. The first one is diet (because families tend to eat the same things!). The second one has to do with the types of bacteria in your intestines. (Remember, these are the bacteria that produce gas while they're helping with digestion.) Not everyone has the same types of bacteria in their intestines. But in a family, the kids will tend to develop the same types as their parents. *(Thanks, Dad!!)* This means that the smell and frequency of farts might be similar too!!

Another thing that can have a major effect on your digestion and 'wind' production is the part of the world you live in. For example, if you live in a warmer country like Greece, you will probably eat lots of fresh fish, fruits and vegetables, and less heavier foods like potatoes, red meat and eggs. This will not only alter the frequency of your butt blasts, but the odour as well!

So ... if families eat similar things and have similar bacteria, how come there are still some members who have **€HFF (€xtra High Farting Frequency)**? Well, extended family members (like uncles, aunts, grandparents and cousins) won't always live in the same house, so they will probably eat different foods. And then there are those families who *encourage* other members to LET RIP anywhere, anytime, because they find it extremely funny!!! (*Awwwww, Uncle Don!!!!*)

FAMILY FUME FIZZER GUIDE

Grandad (Pop) When Pop Goes POP! Grandad loves to fart at any opportunity. He doesn't care who's there, how loud it is, or what the smell is like! At his age, he thinks it's his right to let rip and other family members should revel in his bottom percussion as a sign of respect. Pop has earned the right to POP!

Grandma Grandma has something I like to call 'Nana's manners'. She only launches a butt bomb if she can do it discreetly and without offending anyone. But Grandma does love her cakes (which are full of eggs!) and she knows the value of eating broccoli and cabbage … So even though she will only sneak one out when no one is watching, it might be a little smelly! (Naughty Nana!)

Great Grandad Great Grandad (or Great Grand*pop!*) definitely knows how to POP! He has completely done away with any farting etiquette. He loves to let them rip like there's no tomorrow (and at his age that could be true!). Unlike Great Grandma, the chances are Great Grandad won't be harbouring any ancient secret gases in his tummy, because he has already let them rip at every opportunity! Great Grandad thinks that farting loud and proud is a great health tonic. So, as long as he still has breath (or should that be *gas!*) inside him, Great Grandpop will keep on popping!

Great Grandma Great Grandma, bless her cotton socks, is usually a fairly elderly women who has seen and done it all. You don't get to be that old by luck alone, so regular windy pops will be a vital part of Great Grandma's secret for a long life. But I'm sure she still has some ancient gas pockets hidden away inside her tummy that are harbouring the stinkiest gasses known to mankind … Like prehistoric dinosaurs' fossils, these ancient gases would be EXTREMELY smelly if released … So stay upwind from Great Grandma if possible!!

Uncle Uncles are famous for getting you to pull their finger and then letting one rip! Most uncles think they are allowed to be a little naughty. They try to connect with the kids in the family by acting like the biggest kid of all! But because they are grown-ups, they rarely get in trouble. So beware of your uncle's tricks, like The Big Bad Stinky Stink Bomb! Or dropping a butt bomb in the room and then blaming you!! For these reasons, uncles should be treated with extreme caution!

Aunty Aunties tend to be more discreet than uncles when it comes to bottom burps, but they are famous for releasing sneaky little SBDs (Silent But Deadlies!). Beware if you see your aunty suddenly shuffling away from an area in the lounge room … She might have popped one out and doesn't want to be caught in the vicinity of the smell!! To the naked eye, aunties appear not to fart at all … but we know differently! It might be hard to believe that someone as glamorous as your aunty can be sooooo sneaky and smelly, but don't be fooled!! If you suspect her of releasing an SBD, watch her eyes closely … They will dart quickly from side to side to check if anyone noticed her little gassy gift to the family!

Dad Dad has usually been influenced by his father, his beer-drinking mates and more than a few caveman-like behaviours … This means that although he tries hard to be a gentleman, at any moment he might give in to his caveman ways and let out the most thunderous, explosive, Armageddon-like BOTTOM BLAST! If he notices anyone nearby, he will apologise … but is it *really* an apology if he's smiling and trying not to laugh? And if your dad has a den or a study, BEWARE! That's where he'll do his most toxic butt bombs!!! (You gotta love him for it!)

Mum Mums do everything! Many mums work as well as look after a family – they are extremely busy, so they have to use their precious time as wisely as they can. Mums do fart, but they are usually so busy and moving so quickly that no one notices … not even them! If you do a windy pop near your mum, she won't make a fuss – she might just ask you if you need to go to the toilet. But if she hears your father let one rip, she will probably say, *'Pleeeease!* Do you have to do that?' Mums do everything with a minimum of fuss and this applies to farting as well. Their farts are quick and efficient, with no wasted sound or smell. Just like with the groceries, they shop (or should that be *pop?!*) on the bargain side of Family Fumes!

Older brother Big brother is the great white shark of farting! He will fart on you, beside you, in front of you, behind you, downwind of you, upwind of you … In fact, anywhere that's near you! Big brother has no problems at all belting out a butt blast in front of other people. He loves the humour … and the shock value! He is like a fart predator looking for victims that he can inflict his supersonic smelly concoctions on!! His favourite thing in the world is to shock everyone with his grossness and stinkiness, so WATCH OUT!!!

Younger brother Younger brother is like a farty older brother in training! He loves to fart, but mainly because of the humour and naughtiness of it! Little bro enjoys the many different sounds and smells of his bottom burp when he fires one out! He also loves to share this experience with his friends and has been known to sit in groups so they can all fart and laugh together! In fact, his age group is credited with inventing the cupcake fart (see page 233 for a more detailed explanation).

Teenage sister Ahhhh!! Where do I start? We all know teenage sisters can be very complex and emotional. Everything in their life tends to be a Big Drama, and this also applies to farting. Some teenage girls won't even admit they have a bottom, let alone fart! They will never let one go in public and have been known to walk many hundreds of metres out of their way to let one rip. Like aunties, teenage girls are also the masters of the SBD. They have been known to hold in a gassy gut blast for days if they are in a situation that might be embarrassing, but they also have an inborn psychic gift called **ESFP (Extra Sensory Fart Perception)**. This gift not only helps them know *when* to release their gassy little secret, but also how far away people will be and how long the smell will last! **ESFP** serves them well as it almost totally disguises the fact that they fart! But we all know teenage sisters do fart ... They just find it highly embarrassing!! (OMG!!)

Younger sister
Your younger sis is no doubt a giggly little girl who has not really learned that farting in public can be a bit embarrassing or seen as naughty! She probably has a great relationship with her dad, who will play tricks on her and maybe even let one rip for her amusement! She might also like to let little giggly bottom burps out with her best friends so they can all have a laugh. Don't be fooled though – she may be sweet and giggly, but a little sister can be a smelly little BEASTIE disguised in a super-cute giggly package!

WARNING: Don't tickle continuously for fear of squeaky, smelly explosions!!

The baby Babies are well known for being vomiting, poo producing, dribbling, screaming, crying, burping little bundles of joy! Some babies fart a lot and can be a bit smelly, mainly due to their diet of milk and baby food (as well as the amount of air they swallow!). Babies often get patted on the backs to make them burp and they usually fart at the same time. Baby bottom burps can be smelly, but they can often suffer from stomach cramp if they don't get rid of their gas … So fart on, Bubs!!

PULL MY FINGER
Family fart tricks and gags

Family fart jokes and tricks have been around for as long as there's been farting … That means they have been around for as long as people have been butt burping … That means they have been around for as long as people have been on Earth!

The most famous family fart joke is the 'Pull My Finger' gag. This is a favourite with uncles all around the world.

It goes like this – your uncle calls you over to him and says, 'My finger hurts. Would you be able to pull it for me?' Innocently, you grab his finger, but as you pull it he lets out a MASSIVE GASSY GUT GRUNT! Now this is hilarious to some kids, but it can upset the littlies. (Naughty Uncle!)

Here are some more of my favourite family fart tricks and gags …

1 The Perfume Prank

This is a great trick for the girls in the family to play on the boys! Wait until you have a butt bubble almost ready to go, then sit on the inside of your wrist and let fly! Now walk up to someone (your little brother is a good target!) and ask them to smell your new 'perfume' … Watch your little brother's eyes bulge out when he takes in a whiff of the gassy, eggy smell!!! (Hmmm, I wonder … could a fart be classified as a perfume? Maybe a skunk would think so!)

2 The Jar Trap

This is a great trick and works a treat! Grab an empty jar with a lid (a jam jar is perfect). Now, position yourself over the jar and let rip. As soon as you've finished, cover the top of the jar with your hand and then quickly screw on the lid to trap the gas inside. Now you need to find your victim … (A sister or an aunty is always a good bet!) Walk up to them and say, 'Hey, check out what I just caught in a jar!' Wait until they have bent in really close to the jar and then sloooowly open the lid … Watch and laugh as they get a nostril-thrilling wake-up call!!!

3 The Cupcake

This sounds very sweet and lovely, but don't be deceived!
The cupcake is a mean, sneaky little trick … When you
feel the need to let rip, sneak up next to someone in your
family. Make a cup shape with your hand and quickly fart
into it. Now bring your hand up and cup your victim's
nose … Even if they try not to smell it, it will seep into
their nostrils and show them why you are the Stinky
Cupcake King or Queen!

4 The Blanket Bloomf

All you need for this trick is a blanket or a doona.
Spread your blanket out on the floor and drop a butt
bomb in the middle of it. Wrap the blanket up so the
smelly treat is locked inside and quickly walk towards
another family member. Try to open up the blanket
and wrap it around your brother or sister's face in one
movement. This trick takes some practice, but if it's
done correctly your victim will have your sinister scent
locked in their nostrils for hours!

5 The Cramp

If you are running around outside with your family, this trick will work well. After running for a while, you need to stop suddenly and lie down. Hold one leg tightly and say, 'I have a cramp! Quick, help me!!' When your helper comes over, ask them to push your leg up to stretch out your cramp. Wait until your leg gets fairly high and then … blow a raspberry in their direction! The LOUDER the better!

6 The Pillow Popper

This is a great trick to play on your brothers or sisters. Wait until your brother or sister is almost ready to go to bed. While they are in the bathroom brushing their teeth, sneak into their room and 'borrow' their pillow. Sit in the middle of the pillow (get nice and comfy!) and let one rip!!! Replace the pillow (try to make it look like nothing has been touched) and then wish your brother or sister, 'Sweet dreams' as they go to bed … (Works every time!)

7 Who is Taller?

This trick is a blast. Literally! Ask your mum who she thinks is taller – you or your sister. Tell your mum to come a bit closer and you will line up back to back. Wait until you can feel your sister's bottom against yours and then … let one rip!! Guaranteed to make the whole room giggle!

FAMILY FUME FUNNIES

Q: What sound do Grandad's farts make?

A: *Pop!*

Q: What is the best family fart game?

A: *Ping Pong!*

Q: What is your little sister's favourite fart book?

A: *Winnie the Pooh!*

Q: Where is the best place to buy a fart?

A: *A Fart Mart!*

FAMILY FUME FACTS (FFFs!)

FFF1 – The slang name for farting and then running away is 'crop dusting'.

TRUE! Older brothers are famous for 'crop dusting' – they let one rip and then run forward so the people coming up behind them get the full effect of their STINK BOMB! So if you see your brother suddenly break away from the family group by running fast, watch out!!

FFF2 – The slang name for a wet-sounding windy pop is 'squid'.

TRUE! Babies do the most squids because they drink so much liquid! (*Eeeeeeww!!*)

FFF3 – A family of four can collectively fart around 1000 times a day!

FALSE! An average person farts around 12 times per day. That means a family of four will collectively fart around 48 times a day (unless you have an older brother who does more than his fair share of farting!). All those farts produce around 6 litres of gas per day. That equals around 42 litres of gas per week, and 2184 litres of gas per year!!!

FARTY POEMS

Pop Goes POP!

A. JONES

I love my pop

But here's a tip

If you pull his finger

He'll let one RIP!!!

Pull My Finger

A. JONES

Make sure you never linger

When Uncle Tom says, 'Pull my finger'

If you do, you will fall prey

To the loudest, stinkiest trick of the day!

A FART BY ANY OTHER NAME

FART GLOSSARY

See below for a list of my favourite farting words!
If you can think of a fart word that is not in this list
(or you invent a new one!), email me your word at
fartionary@gmail.com

Bigfart a large, hairy ape-like creature that lives in
forests and frightens unsuspecting hikers with its stinky,
tree-rattling farts!

Fart Chart a chart where you can record the number
of farts you do per minute, per hour, per day, per week,
per month and per year!

Fartercise a type of exercise that is done to funky music and involves lots of farting

Farterrific a really really great fart, or a really amazing situation that involved farting

Fart Farm a farm where the main crop is gassy gut blasts!

Fartician a person who counts and studies every type of fart known to humankind

Fartilicious a fart that smells so delicious it's almost good enough to eat!

Fartinarian a doctor who specialises in animal farts

Fartionary a funny, factual book about everything to do with farting

Fartist an artist who makes art from farts!

Fart Ness Monster a creature that lives in a lake in Scotland and is always surrounded by enormous, sulfur-smelling bubbles!

Fartocrisy when a person says they think farting in public is disgusting, but then they do it all the time!

Fartograph a photo of a fart in motion

Fartoholic a person who is addicted to farting – they fart anywhere, anytime and in front of anyone!

Fartologist a person who studies farts and farting

Fartology the study of farts and farting

Fartometrist a person who studies the effects of farting on eyesight

Fartonics a branch of science and technology that deals with farts and electricity

Fartopia a place where every fart is free, happy and loved by all

Fartopolis an ancient city where people worshipped farting

Fartosaurus a dinosaur (now extinct) that was famous for doing the most enormous farts the world had ever seen!

Farty Claus this person looks like Santa but instead of presents he likes to give people the gift of his super stinky gut gas!

Farty-lingual a person who can 'speak' in farts (and also understands many different types of farts)

Farty Pants a name given to people (usually kids) who fart a lot and aren't ashamed of it!

Farty Party a party where everyone in attendance farts for fun!

Frankenfarter a relative of Frankenstein who loved to blow off everywhere he went!

Frankfart a place in Germany where farts smell like fresh sausages!

FART NAMES FROM A TO Z ...

A

Aftershocks

Air attack

Air biscuit

Air monkey

B

Babbling bottom

Back blast

Back blow

Backdoor trumpet

Back-draft

Back-end bloomp

Backfire

Barking spider

Bean bomb

Bean-town comet

Beep your horn

Blanket bomb

Blanket ripper

Blast the chair

Blow fish

Blow kisses

Blow the butt trumpet

Blow your horn

Blurter

Bottom backfire

Bottom bark

Bottom blast

Bottom blurp

Bottom bubble

Bottom burp

Botty banger

Botty bomb

Botty cough

Break wind

Breezer

Brown haze

Bubbler

Burp out the wrong end

Butt bang

Butt bark

Butt bomb

Butt bouquet

Butt burp

Butt mutt

Butt trumpet

Butt yodeller

C

Cabbage cough

Carpet creeper

Cheek bubble

Cheek sneak

Cheek squeak

Chemical warfare

Colon call

Colon cocktail

Colon croak

Crop dusting

Cushion bleeter

Cut a stinker

Cut loose

Cut the cheese

D

Dinkle doofer

Doona lifter

Drop a beast

Drop your guts

Duck doo doo

E

Emission

Eruption

Evacuation constipation

Explosion

F

Fat fart

Fire in the hole

Flabber-gasser

Flabbergaster

Flatulence

Flatus

Fluff

Fluff thrower

Fluffer

Floopy

Flurpy

Fog horn

Foo foo

Funky roller

G

Gas gurgler

Gas guzzer

Gasser

Gut buster

Gut gas gush

Gut gasser

H

Hind hotpot

Honker

Hurricane

K

Kaboom

L

Let a little bean be heard

Let one go

Let one rip

Low flying duck

M

Machine gun

Methane monster

Mish mush

Morning thunder

Mud slapper

O

One gun salute

P

Pants puffer

Pass gas

Pass wind

Poo-fume

Pop tart

Puff puff

Putt putt

R

Raspberry

Raspberry tart

Rectum honk

Rectum rattler

Rectum ripper

Rectum roar

Rip-snorter

Rotten egg

Rump roar

Rump ripper

S

Silent But Deadly (SBD)

Silent But Friendly (SBF)

Silent But Violent (SBV)

Smelly smoofa

Sphincter whistle

Squeaker

Squeaky deaky

Squiffer

Step on a duck

Step on a toad

Stinker

T

Taco torpedo

Thunder down under

Toot toot

Tooters

Trouser cough

Trouser trumpet

Trumpet blower

W

Wet one

Wind

Wind warning

Windy pop

Y

Yelping spider

About the author

ANDY JONES was found as a tiny baby in a village called Fartopia, lying under a cabbage and wrapped in toilet paper. He was adopted by a family with five smelly boys, the oldest being the most stinky. Andy attended the Fume Primary School and received numerous gas-mask awards for 'bravery in the face of stench'. His adopted mother and farter were legendary fartologists at the Institute of Frankfart. Andy decided to follow in his parents' fart-steps and became a leading fartologist, specialising in disgusting gastrology and gruesome gastronomy. Andy currently farts his way around Australia with his shows 'Electric Music', 'Kam-o-Kidz', 'Andy Jones and the Funky Monkey' and 'What's the Joke?'. These shows contain no farting but they are still very funny!*

* All of the above is 100% true (except for the bits that aren't!).

About the illustrator

DAVID PUCKERIDGE, illustrator and big fartypants, was born in the Windy Pines hospital for the chronically flatulent. After graduating from high school, he attended Honkingbottom Smellyversity. He has illustrated several books, including *The Da Stinky Code*, *Eat Pray Fart*, and *1001 Farts You Must Hear Before You Die*.*

* Some or all of the above may not be the exact 100% truth!

Also by Andy Jones

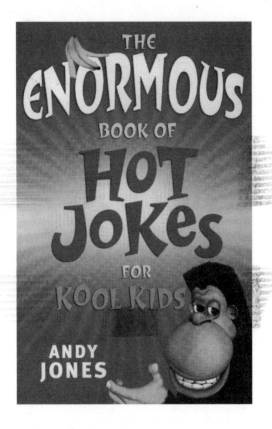

With hundreds of the hottest jokes, rhymes and riddles, this is the ultimate joke book for Kool Kids everywhere!

Turn the page for a sneak peek ...

Thundering Underwear

Bloomers and boxers
Undergarments with flair
There is nothing as silly
As Thundering Underwear

Q   What type of undies do scarecrows wear?

A   **Wicker knickers**   Nicholas F. aged 7

Q   What kind of underwear do bees wear?

A   **Underbear**   Tyson P. aged 9

Q   What type of undies do teachers wear?

A   **Und-Ds**   Christian J. aged 8

Q   What type of underwear packs a punch?

A   **Boxer shorts**   Tina W. aged 9

Q   What never sleeps and constantly needs changing?

A   **A nappy**   Stan D. aged 9

Q   What do baby crabs wear?

A   **Nippy nappies**   Zoe Y. aged 8

Q   What did one pair of underpants say to the other?

A   **I need a change**   Kimberley R. aged 9

Q   What is a musician's favourite undergarment?

A   **A G-string**   Laura P. aged 9

Q   What is the best day of the week to change your underwear?

A   **Mundie**   Kenneth C. aged 7

Body Parts

Double chins
And beating hearts
Piece 'em together
Body Parts

Q   Why did the lady put lipstick on her head?

A   **Because she wanted to make-up her mind**   Gabriella B. aged 10

Q   What do you call a sticky knee?

A   **Hon-ey**   Liam F. aged 5

Q   What type of knee can you get at a bank?

A   **Mon-ey**   Ben H. aged 5

Q   What do you call a knee which tells jokes?

A   **Fun-ny**   Madeleine L. aged 10

Q   What type of room can you fit in your mouth?

A   **A mushroom**   Daniel S. aged 8

Q What type of lids do you wear on your face?

A **Eyelids**   Samuel T. aged 9

Q What type of band can't play music?

A **A hair band**   Prashad T. aged 8

Q What type of stick can you put on your face?

A **Lipstick**   Genevieve K. aged 7

Q What do you call a baby knee?

A **A mini**   Rhiannon L. aged 7

Q What type of cage has no bars?

A **A rib cage**   Joanne S. aged 9

Q What do you call beautiful hands?

A **Hand-some**   Kayla S. aged 8

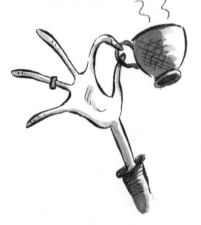